Silken Eyes

ALSO BY FRANÇOISE SAGAN

FICTION
Bonjour Tristesse
A Certain Smile
Those Without Shadows
Aimez-vous Brahms ...
The Wonderful Clouds
The Heart Keeper
La Chamade
Sunlight on Cold Water
Scars on the Soul
Lost Profile

NONFICTION
Tozique

DRAMA
Chateau en Suede

Silken Eyes

Françoise Sagan

Translated from the French
by JOANNA KILMARTIN

DELACORTE PRESS/ELEANOR FRIEDE

Published by
Delacorte Press/Eleanor Friede
1 Dag Hammarskjold Plaza
New York, New York 10017

Originally published in French by Librairie Ernest Flammarion
under the title Des Yeux de Soie. Copyright © 1975 by Flammarion.

Copyright © 1977 by Andre Deutsch Ltd. and Dell Publishing Co., Inc.

Manufactured in the United States of America
First U.S.A. printing
Designed by MaryJane DiMassi

Library of Congress Cataloging in Publication Data

Sagan, Françoise, 1935–
    Silken eyes.
    Translation of Des yeux de soie.
    CONTENTS: Silken eyes.—The gigolo.—In extremis.
{etc}
    I.   Title.
PZ4.Q9Si   {PQ2633.U74}   843'.9'14   77-21659

ISBN 0-440-08308-7

Contents

Silken Eyes   *1*

The Gigolo   *21*

In Extremis   *33*

The Unknown Visitor   *43*

The Five Diversions   *55*

The Gentlemanly Tree   *61*

An Evening Out   *69*

A Stylish Death   *75*

The Fishing Expedition   *85*

Death in Espadrilles   *91*

The Left Eyelid   *103*

A Dog's Night   *121*

Separation Roman-style   *129*

The Corner Café   *141*

The Seven O'Clock Fix   *149*

Italian Skies   *155*

The Sun Also Sets   *167*

The Lake of Loneliness   *173*

Silken Eyes

JEROME BERTHIER WAS DRIVING HIS CAR TOO FAST,
and it required all the cool indifference at his beautiful
wife Monika's command to ignore the risks he took. They
were setting off for a weekend's stalking in Bavaria,
something that was a real pleasure trip for him, since he
loved hunting, and his wife, and the mountains and even
the friends they were on their way to pick up—Stanislas
Brem and his current girl friend (he'd had a new one
practically every couple of weeks since his divorce).

"I hope they'll be ready," said Jerome. "What sort of
girl do you think he'll produce for us this time?"

Monika smiled wearily.

"How should I know? I only hope she's the sporting type. The hunt will be tough going, won't it?"

He nodded.

"Very tough. I must say, I wonder what Stanislas thinks he's up to, showing off to girls at his age, *our* age. . . . In the meantime, if he's not ready, we're going to miss the plane."

"You never miss anything," she said with a laugh.

Jerome Berthier glanced at his wife out of the corner of his eye and wondered, not for the first time, what she meant. He was a stolid, virile, confident man. He knew he was not unattractive, and for the thirteen years of their marriage he had provided this beautiful woman—the only woman he had ever loved—with a completely secure, thoroughly pleasant life. Still, there were times when he wondered what lay behind that calm exterior and those tranquil dark eyes.

"What do you mean?" he asked.

"I mean that you never miss anything at all, in your business or in your private life. You won't miss your plane and I very much doubt if you'll miss your chamois, either."

"I sincerely hope not," he said. "I don't go shooting in order to lose by chance, and believe me, it's the most difficult animal of all to stalk."

They had arrived in front of an apartment house complex in the Boulevard Raspail, and Jerome had to blow the

horn three times before a window opened and a man
appeared, waving his arms in welcome. Jerome stuck his
head out of the car window and yelled:

"Come on down, old boy. We'll miss the plane."

The window closed, and two minutes later Stanislas
Brem and a girl emerged from the hallway.

Stanislas Brem was as suggestible, high-strung and
lanky as Jerome was strong-minded, calm and compact.
The girl was blonde and extremely pretty, with a slightly
wary look about her—a typical weekend date. They
climbed into the back of the car and Stanislas made the
introductions.

"Monika, my dear, may I present Betty? Betty, meet
Monika and her husband, Jerome Berthier, the famous
architect. From now on you're under his orders—he's our
skipper."

Everyone laughed politely, and Monika shook hands in a
friendly way with the girl. Jerome drove off in the
direction of Charles de Gaulle airport. Stanislas leaned
forward and asked in a rather high-pitched voice:

"Well, glad to be off, you two?"

Without waiting for a reply, he turned back to Betty
and smiled at her. He was extremely attractive in an
obvious way, slightly decadent, a bit of a playboy and a
man who enjoyed pursuing attractive women. And Betty
smiled back at him, seemingly enchanted.

"Just think," he went on at the top of his voice, "I've known this man for twenty years. We were at school together. And Jerome was always the best at everything. He swung the hardest punch of the lot in the playground —often in my defense, too, because I was insufferable even in those days."

And then, pointing toward Monika:

"I've known her for thirteen years. They're a happy couple, my dear, take a good look at them."

In front, neither Jerome nor Monika appeared to be listening. Faint, almost conspiratorial smiles hovered about their lips.

"And when I got divorced," Stanislas went on, "they were the ones who consoled me in my misery."

The car was traveling so fast along the highway that Betty had to shout her question:

"Why were you so miserable? Didn't your wife love you anymore?"

"No!" yelled Stanislas in reply, "*I* didn't love *her* anymore, and, believe me, for a gentleman that's an appalling situation."

He roared with laughter and flung himself back on the seat cushion.

And then they were at the airport, the hell of Roissy, and admiring Jerome's efficiency as he presented their

tickets, checked their baggage, took charge of everything.
The three others looked on, the women taking it for
granted that a man should look after them, and Stanislas
seeming to make it a point of honor not to lift a finger.
Then they were on the moving ramps, where they filed
past under the plastic domes two by two, standing as
though frozen to the spot, prepackaged models of the
affluent couples of our time. Then they were in the plane,
in first class, one couple behind the other, and Monika
watched the clouds drift past the window without even
bothering to flick through the magazine in her lap.
Toward the end of an hour Jerome left his seat, and
suddenly, there, close to her, was Stanislas' profile, his
hand apparently pointing to something out of the
window, but his voice saying:

"I want you, you know; you fix it, I don't care when, but
I want you this weekend."

She blinked but made no reply.

"Tell me it's what you want, too," he went on, still
smiling.

She turned toward him, looked at him gravely, but
before she could say anything the loudspeaker announced:
"We are about to land at Munich airport. Please return to
your seats. Fasten your seat belts and no further smoking,
please." Their eyes met for a moment, like enemies or

lovers or both, and he smiled, meaning it this time, and
settled back in his seat. Jerome returned to his place
beside her.

It was raining buckets. They had hired a car to get to the
shooting lodge, and naturally Jerome was the driver.
Before getting into the car, Monika politely asked the
newcomer, Betty, whether she suffered from car sickness.
Betty, who seemed to be starved for civilized behavior and
respectability, nodded, and was seated in front, beside
Jerome.

Jerome was in the best of spirits. With the downpour, the
fallen leaves, the patches of fog, he had to concentrate on
the road, but his control of headlights and windshield
wipers and the purr of the engine interposed a sort of wall
between him and the others that was not disagreeable. As
usual, he was conscious of being the man in charge, the
pilot of this little spacecraft that was taking them to their
destination. He steered, accelerated, braked and guided
four lives including his own, with a sense of familiarity
and complete confidence. The turns were very sharp, and
it was already pitch-dark. The road was hemmed in by
larch and fir trees and tumbling streams. Through the
window Jerome inhaled all the traditional scents of
autumn. No doubt because of the twisting and turning,
Stanislas and Monika had stopped talking. He glanced
back over his shoulder.

"Not asleep? Betty's almost snoring."

Stanislas laughed.

"No, we're not asleep. We're just looking, looking at the dark."

"How about some music?"

He switched on the radio and instantly the car was filled with the fabulous voice of Montserrat Caballé. She was singing the great aria from *Tosca*, and to his intense surprise Jerome felt his eyes fill with tears, so much so that he had automatically started the windshield wipers before realizing that it wasn't the autumn weather that was blurring his vision. Suddenly he thought: I love this weather, I love this country, I love this road, I love this car and, above all, I love this woman behind me, this dark-haired woman who's mine and who shares my pleasure in this other woman's singing.

Jerome confided little to anyone, spoke little—still less to others than to himself. People said of him that he was a plain, almost brutal man; but now, suddenly, he felt an urge to stop the car, get out, open the rear door, take his wife in his arms and, no matter how silly it looked, tell her that he loved her. The singer's voice soared effortlessly, the orchestra lagging behind as though hypnotized, bemused by that voice; and Jerome, almost overcome by emotion—a term not normally associated with him—tilted the rearview mirror and glanced at his wife. He expected to see her as he so often saw her at concerts, motionless, transfixed, wide-eyed, but he had bent the mirror too forcefully and what he saw was Stanislas' long, thin hand lying palm to palm in Monika's. He quickly readjusted the mirror and the music became an incoherent and incomprehensible series of hideous sounds, bawled out by a madwoman. For a brief moment he could hardly see the road or the trees or the oncoming bend. But all at once the responsible man of action within him corrected the swerve of the wheel, touched the brakes, and just as calmly decided that the man behind him, the blond, blue-eyed man crouched beside his wife in the dark, had to die—by tomorrow night and by his own hand. The swerve had not gone unnoticed by the man in question, and immediately the now hateful, loathsome face of his childhood friend was close to his.

"Hey!" said Stanislas. "Are you dreaming?"

"No," he replied, "I was listening to *Tosca.*"

"Ah, *Tosca!*" said Stanislas cheerfully. "Where have they got to?"

"They've reached the point where Scarpia decides to kill Mario out of jealousy."

"And quite right, too," said Stanislas with a laugh. "It's the only thing to do."

He settled back next to Monika, and Jerome at once felt a sense of profound relief. The wild, raging chorus of

voices on the radio died away and he smiled to himself.
It was indeed the only thing to do.

The hunting lodge was large, built of birchwood, with
beamed ceilings, animal-skin rugs and, mounted on the
walls, the stuffed heads of the most handsome of the
victims. An appropriate setting indeed! Suddenly he found
it grotesque. He had waked Betty, unloaded the luggage,
lit the fires and asked the housekeeper to prepare a meal.
They had dined in high spirits, listening—a whim of
Stanislas'—to American songs on the old-fashioned
phonograph. Now he and Monika were in their bedroom:
she was undressing in the adjoining bathroom and he was
sitting on the end of the bed, finishing off a bottle of
Wilhelmina.

He felt within himself a sense of unutterable misery and
pain. He knew he couldn't bring himself to ask her: "Is it
true? Since when? Why? How will it end?" It was a very
long time, in fact, since he had talked to his wife. He took
her everywhere, gave her everything, made love to her, but
he no longer talked to her. And in a confused way he felt
that questions like these, however justified, would merely
have seemed tactless, gauche, almost vulgar.

He drank steadily, for no special reason, not even out of
despair. He drank to calm himself. He wasn't a man
given to sleeping pills or amphetamines. He wasn't a

man given to anything. *A simple man*, he thought bitterly, with a kind of derision and self-contempt.

Monika came back into the room, her hair as dark, her cheekbones as high, her eyes as tranquil as they had always been. Passing him, she put her hand on his head in that habitual gesture she had, which was a sign of both tenderness and power, and he didn't recoil from her touch.

"You look tired," she said. "You ought to be in bed. You've got to make an early start in the morning."

It was odd, when you came to think of it: she never went stalking, never wanted to come out with them. She claimed that the noise of a gun going off frightened her, that the excitement of the dogs upset her; she just didn't like shooting. It had never occurred to him to wonder what the real reason was; after all, it wasn't as though she minded getting tired or walking long distances, and she had never been frightened of anything.

"It's odd," he said, and his voice suddenly sounded thick in his ears, "it's odd that you never come out with us."

She laughed.

"You're surprised, after ten years?"

"It's never too late," he said stupidly, and to his surprise he suddenly began to blush.

"Of course it is," she said, lying back and yawning. "Of course it's too late. Anyway, I love wild animals; I find them more dignified than the other kind."

"Dignified?" he said.

She smiled and switched off her bedside light.

"Oh, never mind," she said, "I don't know what I mean. Why don't you come to bed?"

Obediently he took off his sweater and shoes, and flopped down on the other side of the bed.

"Lazybones!" she said, and leaning across him switched off the light on his side.

He listened, hearing only silence. She was breathing quietly, on the brink of sleep.

"Didn't you think," he asked, and his voice seemed to him as hesitant and anxious as a child's, "didn't you think Caballé sang that aria from *Tosca* well?"

"Yes," she said, "beautifully. Why?"

There was a moment's silence, then she laughed: that familiar laugh of hers, low-pitched, light, natural.

"The opera's made you romantic, or the autumn, or both."

He leaned over and fumbled on the floor for the bottle of Wilhelmina. The alcohol was cold and hot and odorless.

I could turn round, take her in my arms, make her do anything I liked, he told himself. And someone within him, someone childish, weak, famished, stretched out a hand toward her. He touched her shoulder, and with a gesture that was completely natural, she moved her head and pressed her lips to his hand.

"Go to sleep," she said. "It's late. I'm exhausted, and so will you be in the morning. Go to sleep, Jerome."

He took his hand away then, and turned over on his other side; and the frightened child disappeared and gave place to a forty-year-old man who lay in the dark, ice-cold and inflamed with Wilhelmina, meticulously, painstakingly working out the way in which, thanks to a telescopic sight, a gun barrel, a trigger, shot, shell and blast, he could eliminate from life, and above all from the life of this stranger at his side, a blond and dangerous enemy called Stanislas.

It was ten o'clock in the morning. The weather was beautiful, unbearably beautiful. They had been beating the woods for three hours. The gamekeeper had spotted a superb chamois, and Jerome had twice had it in his binoculars, but at present he had quite another quarry in mind. His intended quarry had fair hair, a fawn suede and doeskin outfit and was peculiarly difficult to kill. He had already missed him twice. The first time the other had darted with one bound behind a bush, having imagined he'd seen the chamois. The second time Betty's blonde head had interposed itself between the shimmering black dot and his prey. But now he had him well and truly lined up. Stanislas Brem was standing in the middle of a clearing. With his gun resting between his feet, his weight on one leg, he was gazing up at the blue sky and the russet trees with a kind of insufferable contentment. Jerome's finger tightened on the trigger. That profile was about to be blown to smithereens, those silky, degenerate blond locks would never again be smoothed by Monika's hand, those corrupt boyish looks were about to be shattered by a bullet. Then suddenly, unexpectedly, with the gesture of a man who knows he is alone, Stanislas raised his arms to the sky; letting his gun fall to the ground, he stretched himself in a voluptuous and abandoned way.

As though he had been slapped in the face, Jerome fired. Stanislas gave a start and looked around him, seemingly more astonished than frightened. Jerome lowered his gun, noticing, without the least pride, that his hands weren't trembling, but noticing also, with fury, that he had forgotten to adjust the sight. He had been aiming at a target six hundred feet away with the sight set for one-quarter that distance. He corrected it, put the gun to his shoulder and was more irritated than alarmed to hear the keeper say:

"Did you see something, Monsieur Berthier?"

"I thought I did," said Jerome, turning round.

"You mustn't let your gun off, sir," said the keeper. "If

you want that chamois, you mustn't make a noise. I know where he's headed, I know where we can corner him. We mustn't scare him off."

"Sorry," said Jerome stupidly. "I won't loose off like that again."

And he unloaded his gun and followed the old man.

He was oddly torn between amusement and annoyance. He knew for a certainty that he would kill Stanislas before the day was out, but he was beginning to take pleasure in spinning it out.

Two hours later, he was lost. In fact, they were all lost; the chamois was too cunning, the forest too vast, the beaters too few. Because he was stalking another, unofficial quarry, it was Jerome who, quite alone, happened upon the chamois; but it was a long way, a very long way, off. It was perched on a rock, silhouetted against the sun, absolutely motionless. Instinctively, Jerome reached for his binoculars. His hands were trembling now; he was growing tired and short of breath. He was getting old, he was forty years old and he loved a woman who no longer loved him. For a second this thought almost blinded him, then he refocused his binoculars and saw the chamois in close-up, so near it seemed he could touch it. It was young and tawny, its eyes were anxious but proud, and its gaze moved back and forth between the

direction of the mountain and the direction of the valley
from which its enemies approached; it seemed to be
mocking this death hunt. There was something timorous,
fragile yet invulnerable, about it. Its very presence attested
to the charm of innocence, agility and flight. It was
beautiful, the most beautiful creature Jerome had ever
stalked.

"That man can wait," Jerome said to himself. "I'll kill
him later." (He could no longer even remember his
name.) "But now, my beauty, it's you I want."

And he began to climb the terrifyingly steep track that
would take him to the chamois.

Below him, the stalking party was in disarray. There was
the sound of dogs barking from all directions and of
whistles growing fainter and fainter, and Jerome felt that
he was putting the sordid, dreary world behind him and
returning to his true element.

In spite of the sun, it was very cold. When he raised his
binoculars again, the chamois was still there. It seemed to
be watching him, then trotted off into a clump of trees.
Jerome reached the clump an hour later. He followed the
tracks to the mouth of a gorge and there, once again, the
chamois was waiting for him. They were the only ones left
in the chase. Jerome's heart was beating furiously and he
felt like vomiting. He sat down for a moment before

starting off again. Then he stopped to eat some bread and ham from his game bag, and the chamois waited for him, or so it seemed. Now it was four o'clock in the afternoon and he had gone beyond the limits of the shoot and almost beyond the limits of his strength. The chamois was always there ahead of him, fugitive, fragile, but always visible in its beauty through the lenses of his binoculars. Out of range, of course, and out of reach, but still there.

Jerome was now so tired, after eight hours of pursuing or following—he no longer knew which—this strange creature, that he found himself talking out loud. He had christened the chamois "Monika," and from time to time as he went along, stumbling and uttering the grossest obscenities, he would say: "For God's sake, Monika, don't go so fast!" Once, coming to a swamp, he hesitated, then calmly waded in, holding his gun above his head, up to his waist in water, dangerous and stupid though he knew it to be for a man out stalking alone in this weather. And then, he felt himself slip; at first he let himself go. He went over backwards, losing his foothold, the water up to his neck, in his mouth and nose, half suffocating him. He was overcome by an inexpressible relief, a relief at abandoning the struggle that was so foreign to his nature. I'm committing suicide, he thought, and the sober man within him took charge once more, brought him back to his senses and dragged him, soaked and pale and shivering, out of that wretched swamp. He was reminded of something—what was it? He began to talk out loud:

"When I was listening to Caballé I felt as though I were about to drown, that I *was* drowning. It's like that time, do you remember, the first time I told you I loved you? We were at your place, and you came up to me, and—do you remember?—it was the first time we made love together. I was so frightened of making love to you and at the same time so longing to, I felt as though I were about to commit suicide."

He groped for the brandy flask in his game bag, which was stuffed now with soaked and useless cartridges, and took a long pull. Then he raised his binoculars, and there, still just ahead of him, was the chamois—Monika—the love (he no longer knew its name) that awaited him. Thank God, his gun was loaded and still dry.

By five o'clock, the autumn sun was low on the horizon. Jerome's teeth were chattering as he started up the final gully. He was exhausted and lay down in a patch of sunlight. Monika came and sat beside him and he went on with his monologue:

"And do you remember that time we quarreled and you wanted to leave me? It was about ten days before we were to be married, I think; I was lying on the lawn, at your parents' house, and the weather was awful and I was miserable. I'd closed my eyes, I remember clearly now, and suddenly I felt the warmth of the sun on my eyelids, and it was like a miracle: the weather had been so bad until then, and when I opened my eyes on account of the sun, you were sitting there, or rather kneeling, beside me, and you were looking at me and smiling."

"Oh, yes," she said. "I remember very well. You had been unspeakable, and I was absolutely furious. After a bit, I went to look for you, and when I saw you lying on the grass sulking, it made me want to laugh and kiss you."

Whereupon she vanished, and rubbing his eyes, Jerome got to his feet. At the head of the gorge there was a clifflike rock, steep, almost vertical, in front of which the chamois stood without moving. Jerome had cornered his prey. He had earned it. Never before had he spent nearly ten hours in pursuit of any game, bird or beast. He paused, exhausted, at the foot of the final incline, and cocked his gun. The chamois, now no more than sixty-five feet away, looked at him. It was as beautiful as ever, slightly sweat-stained, and its blue-yellow eyes, its silken eyes, stared unblinkingly.

Jerome raised his gun and took aim, at which the chamois did something foolish and clumsy: it turned away and, no doubt for the tenth time, tried to scale the rock face, and, no doubt for the tenth time, it slipped, skidded awkwardly despite its natural grace and ended up standing stock-still, trembling but still defiant, face to face with Jerome's gun.

Jerome never knew why, when or how he decided not to kill the chamois. Perhaps it was because of the creature's clumsy and despairing effort, perhaps its simple beauty, perhaps the pride and passive animality in the slanting eyes. Jerome never asked himself why.

He turned and retraced his steps along the same untrodden path, back to the hunting lodge. He found the others in a state of panic; they had looked for him everywhere, even the gamekeeper, who, he sensed, knew. Nevertheless, when they asked him where the chamois was and where he had given up the chase—for he had arrived half blind, stiff and sick with exhaustion before collapsing on the threshold—he didn't know what to reply.

Stanislas brought him a brandy, and his wife, sitting on the bed, close to him, held his hand. She looked pale. He asked her why, and she replied that she had been frightened for him. To his surprise, he believed her at once.

"You were afraid I'd be killed," he said, "that I'd fall off a rock?"

She nodded without answering, then impulsively leaned over and laid her head on his shoulder. It was the first time in her life that she had been demonstrative toward him in public. Stanislas, returning with another glass of brandy, took in the scene, stunned: the woman's dark hair on the exhausted man's shoulder, and her gentle sobs, sobs of relief. Suddenly, Stanislas threw the glass of brandy into the fireplace.

"Tell me," he said, and his voice had become strident, "what about the chamois? Couldn't you even manage to carry your kill home on your back, a tough guy like you?"

And then, before the blazing fire, and before the astonished Betty, Jerome Berthier, to his own amazement, heard himself say:

"It wasn't that. I just couldn't bring myself to kill it."

Monika lifted her head a moment and they looked at each other. Slowly she put out a hand and caressed his face lightly with her fingers.

"You know," she said (and at that moment they were alone in the world), "you know, even if you had killed it . . ."

And to all intents and purposes the others disappeared, and he pulled her close to him, and the flames of the fire leaped up to unprecedented heights.

The Gigolo

HE WALKED BESIDE HER ALONG THE RAIN-SODDEN
paths full of dead leaves, giving her his hand now and
again to guide her around a puddle. He smiled as he did
so, a genuine, unforced smile. It occurred to her that this
walk in the woods around Meudon would have been a
penance for any young man, especially with a woman of
her age. Not an old woman, but a bored, jaded one who
walked through the woods without any real pleasure,
merely because it was preferable to the cinema or a
crowded bar.

Of course, for him there had been the drive there, in the
luxurious fast car which it gave him a childish pleasure to
drive; but was that sufficient compensation for this

interminable silent walk along these desolate autumnal paths? "He's bored, he must be bored to death." Strangely relishing the idea, she turned down another path, one that led them further away from the car, with a sort of dread mixed with hope—hope that he would suddenly revolt against this boredom, lose his temper, say something wounding, unforgivable, anything that would justify the gap of more than twenty years between them.

But he always smiled. She had never known him irritable or rude, never seen him smirk in the condescending way of very young men who know they are desirable. The smirk that said so plainly: "All right, as a favor to you . . . But remember, I'm as free as air: so don't irritate me." The cruel smirk of youth that had made her cold, hard and wounding, and had so often caused her to end an affair. With Michel, for instance, in whom she had first noticed it, then with the others . . .

"Careful," he said, taking her arm, saving her from tearing her stockings or her dress, her well-cut, elegant dress, on a bramble. If he should ever smirk like that, would she still be able to throw him out like the rest of them? She didn't feel she would have the heart. Not that she respected him more than the others: she kept him completely, dressed him, gave him expensive presents that he didn't throw back in her face. He never attempted

those stupid, boorish ploys the others indulged in, the
sulky moods when they wanted something or felt they
were the injured party in the bargain struck between their
bodies and her money—that was it, really: they felt taken
advantage of. They would get her to buy them all manner
of luxuries and expensive trinkets that they didn't even
want, solely to restore their self-esteem. The word
"esteem" made her laugh inwardly. It was nonetheless
the only word for it.

Perhaps Nicholas' charm lay in the fact that he really
longed for these presents; not that he demanded them,
but he took such evident pleasure in receiving them that
she felt like a normal woman rewarding a child instead of
an aging mistress buying a fresh young body she secretly
despised. She quickly dismissed such thoughts. Thank God,
she didn't go in for being maternal and protective with
that pack of grasping young men who were too handsome
for their own good. Neither did she disguise the facts; she
was cynical and clearheaded, and they knew it and
respected her for it, however grudgingly. "You give me
your body, I pay you for it." Some, piqued at not having
to rebuff her, had tried to introduce a vague touch of
sentimentality, perhaps in order to get a little more out of
her. These she had sent to other protectresses, explaining
to them exactly where they stood: "I despise you, as I

depise myself for putting up with you. I only keep you for the sake of those two hours at night." She reduced them to the level of pets, deliberately, without a qualm.

With Nicholas, it was not so simple: he brought no trace of affection, or caddishness or sentimentality to his role as gigolo. He was friendly, polite and a good lover— not very expert, perhaps, but passionate, almost tender. . . . He stayed at home all day, lolling about on the carpet, reading anything he could lay his hands on. He didn't ask to be taken out all the time, and when they did go out he seemed to be unaware of the meaningful looks they attracted: he was as attentive and smiling as if he were escorting the young girl of his choice. In fact, apart from the condescension, the brutality, with which she treated him, there was nothing to distinguish their relationship from that of an ordinary couple.

"Aren't you cold?" He glanced at her anxiously as though her health really mattered to him more than anything else in the world. She felt exasperated with him for playing his part so well, for being so nearly what she might still have hoped for ten years ago; she remembered that at that time she still had her rich husband, her rich and boring husband, to whom business was the only thing that mattered.

How could she have been so stupid as to have failed to take advantage of her beauty, now faded, and been unfaithful to him. She had been asleep then, and it had taken her husband's death and her first night with Michel to awaken her. Everything had begun that night.

"I asked you if you were cold."

"No, no. Anyway, it's time we went back."

"Wouldn't you like my jacket?"

His beautiful Creed jacket . . . she glanced at it without interest, as at some dull new possession. A russet and gray check, its autumn colors suited Nicholas' thick, silky auburn hair.

"How autumnal we are," she murmured to herself. "Your jacket, this wood . . . my autumn years . . ."

He didn't reply. She was surprised at herself because she never alluded to her age. He knew perfectly well how old she was and he didn't care. She might just as well throw herself into that lake. She imagined herself, for a moment, floating in the water in her Dior dress. . . . Thoughts like that were all very well for the young. "At my age, one doesn't think of death, one clings to life." One clings to the pleasures of money, of the night; one makes the most of things, and of people, such as a young man walking beside one down a deserted woodland path.

"Nicholas," she said in her husky, imperious voice, "Nicholas, kiss me."

They were separated by a puddle. He looked at her for a moment before stepping over it, and the thought flashed through her mind: He must hate me. He took her in his arms and gently raised her head.

My age, she thought, as he kissed her, just for the moment you've forgotten my age; you're too young to play with fire without getting burned, Nicholas. . . .

"Nicholas!"

He looked at her, a little breathless, his hair rumpled.

"You were hurting me," she said with a faint smile.

They walked on in silence. She was surprised at the quickening of her pulse. That kiss—what had come over Nicholas?—that kiss was like a farewell kiss, hungry and sad, as if he loved her! He was as free as air; women and luxuries were his for the asking. What had possessed him? And that sudden pallor . . . He was dangerous, extremely dangerous. They had been together for over six months; it couldn't go on any longer without leading to trouble. Besides, she was tired, tired of Paris, of the noise and rush. Tomorrow she would leave for the Midi, alone.

They were back at the car. She turned to him and took his arm in an automatic gesture of pity. After all, she thought, the poor boy's losing his livelihood. Even if it's only temporary, it's a nasty blow.

"I'm leaving for the Midi tomorrow, Nicholas. I'm tired."

"Will you be taking me?"

"No, Nicholas, I shan't be taking you."

She almost wished that she were; it would have been fun
showing Nicholas the sea. He must have been there
before, of course, but he always gave the impression of
discovering everything for the first time.

"You've . . . you've had enough of me?"

He spoke softly, his eyes downcast. There was a break in
his voice that touched her. She had a glimpse of the life
he would have, the sordid quarrels, the compromises and
the boredom, all because he was too handsome, too weak,
and the ideal prey for a certain kind of woman belonging
to a certain milieu and with a certain income, women like
herself.

"I haven't had enough of you in the least, my dear
Nicholas. You're very sweet, very attractive, but it couldn't
go on forever, could it? It's over six months since we met."

"I know," he said, as though his mind were elsewhere.
"The first time was at that cocktail party of Mme.
Essini's."

She suddenly remembered that hectic party and the first
glimpse she had had of Nicholas, looking miserable
because old Mme. Essini was talking to him at very close
quarters and giggling girlishly. Nicholas was pressed up
against the bar, with no hope of escape. The scene had
amused her at first, then she had looked at Nicholas with
increasing interest and cynical speculation. These cocktail

parties were like horse fairs or cattle shows. One almost expected to see mature ladies lifting the young men's upper lips to examine their teeth.

Finally, she had gone over to greet her hostess and, passing before a mirror, had suddenly been struck by her own beauty. Nicholas' relief at the interruption had been so obvious that she couldn't help smiling, and her smile had put old Mme. Essini on her guard.

She had introduced Nicholas with reluctance. Then there had been the usual gossip about people and their private lives. Nicholas seemed rather at sea. After an hour, she found him decidedly attractive and resolved to tell him so at once, as was her way. They were sitting on a sofa by a window and he was lighting a cigarette, when she addressed him by name in a voice that scarcely faltered:

"I find you very attractive, Nicholas."

He made no response but took the cigarette out of his mouth and gazed at her.

"I live at the Ritz," she went on coldly.

She was well aware of the importance of this last point. The Ritz was the answer to every gigolo's dream. Nicholas made a slight gesture of protest but said nothing to show that he had understood. She thought, Well, that's that, and rose to her feet.

Nicholas got up, too. He was rather pale.

"May I escort you home?"

In the car, he had put his arm over her shoulders and asked her innumerable eager questions about the overdrive and the finer points of the engine. In the bedroom, it was she who had kissed him first, and he had taken her in his arms with a slight tremor, a mixture of violence and gentleness. At dawn, while he slept like a child, dead to the world, she had gone to the window to watch the day break over the Place Vendôme.

Thereafter, it had been Nicholas playing patience on the floor, Nicholas by her side at the races, Nicholas' eyes on the gold cigarette case she gave him and Nicholas suddenly seizing her hand during a party and kissing it. And now there was Nicholas whom she was about to leave and who said nothing, who was keeping up this pose of exaggerated indifference. . . .

She got into the car and threw her head back, suddenly exhausted. Nicholas got in beside her and drove off.

From time to time on the way back she glanced at his preoccupied, distant profile and could not help thinking that she would have been madly in love with him at twenty and that maybe life was nothing but a hopeless mess. When they reached the Porte d'Italie, Nicholas turned to her:

"Where are we going?"

"We have to drop in at Johnny's Bar," she said. "I've made a date with Mme. Essini there for seven o'clock."

Mme. Essini was punctual as usual. It was one of her few virtues. Nicholas shook the old lady's hand, looking rather distraught.

Watching them both, a pleasing idea came to her:

"By the way, I'm leaving for the Midi tomorrow, so I shan't be able to come to your party on the sixteenth. I'm so sorry."

Mme. Essini regarded them both with a bogus air of affection:

"You lucky things, off to the sun . . ."

"I'm not going," said Nicholas shortly.

There was a silence. The eyes of both women converged on Nicholas, Mme. Essini's the more meaningfully.

"Then you must come to my party. You can't stay in Paris all alone, it's too depressing."

"What a good idea," she interjected.

Mme. Essini's hand was already resting possessively on Nicholas' sleeve. The latter's reaction was unexpected. He jumped up and walked out. She found him waiting by the car.

"What's come over you, Nicholas? Poor old Essini might have been a bit premature, but she's fancied you for a long time; there's nothing to get upset about."

Nicholas stood there without a word and seemed to be breathing with difficulty. She felt an upsurge of pity.

"Get in. You can tell me all about it when we get home."

But he didn't wait until they got home. He told her in a strangled voice that he wasn't an animal to be bought and sold, that he could perfectly well look after himself and that he refused to be put out to pasture with an old vulture like Essini. And in any case he couldn't do anything for her, she was too old. . . .

"But, my dear Nicholas, she's my age."

They had arrived. Nicholas turned toward her and suddenly took her face between his hands. He looked at her searchingly and she tried in vain to free herself, conscious that her makeup had probably not survived the day.

"You're different," said Nicholas in a low voice. "You're . . . you're beautiful. I like your face. How could you . . ."

There was a note of despair in his voice as he let her go. She was dumbfounded.

"How could I what?"

"How could you offer me to that woman? Haven't I spent six months with you? Didn't it occur to you that I might become attached to you, that I could . . . ?"

She turned away brusquely.

"You're cheating," she said in a low voice. "*I* can't afford to cheat. I've had enough. Go away."

Alone in her bedroom, she examined herself in the mirror. She was irretrievably old; she was over sixty and her eyes were full of tears. She packed hurriedly and went to bed alone in her double bed. She cried for some time before going to sleep, putting it down to nerves.

In
Extremis

HE TURNED OVER ONCE AGAIN BETWEEN THE
enveloping sheets, dangerous as quicksand, sniffing with
disgust the smell of his own body, that smell he had once
so delighted to find on women's bodies in the morning.
Those mornings in Paris after a few hours of exhausted
sleep beside a strange body, those mornings when he
awoke light-headed with fatigue and in a hurry to leave.
In a hurry . . . He had always been a man in a hurry, but
now, on this spring afternoon, lying stretched out on his
back, he was taking his time about dying. Dying was a
strange word, no longer the absurd fact of life that had so
often spurred him on, but a sort of accident. Rather like
breaking a leg skiing. Why me? Why today? Why?

"Of course, I may recover," he said out loud. And the shadowy figure silhouetted against the window gave a slight start. He had forgotten her, as indeed he had always forgotten her. He remembered his surprise on learning of her affair with Jean. There was someone for whom she still existed, was still beautiful, for whom she had a body. He gave a faint chuckle that quickened his precious, precarious heartbeat.

He was dying. He knew now that he was dying. Something was tearing at his body. Meanwhile she was leaning over him, supporting him by the shoulders, and he felt his shoulder blade, degradedly reduced to skin and bone, flinch beneath his wife's gentle hand. Ignominy, that was what he was dying of, ignominy. Was there an illness that allowed you to die gracefully? There probably wasn't, and mankind's only grace, perhaps, lay in that aspiration toward what lay ahead. But he was calmer now, and as she leaned over to lay him back on his pillow, her face caught the light and he saw her. A beautiful face, all said and done, for which he had married her twenty years earlier. But its expression irritated him. It was preoccupied, abstracted. She must be thinking of Jean.

"I was saying that I might perhaps recover."

"Of course you will," she said.

It was funny: she really didn't love him anymore. She knew perfectly well that he was lost, done for. But it was such a long time ago that "she" had lost him. "One only loses people once." Where had he read that? Was it true? In any event, she would never again see him come through the door, read his newspaper, talk. No, she no longer loved him. If she had loved him, she would have taken his hands and said: "Yes, my darling, you're going to die," with that smooth, drawn face that comes from knowledge of the irrevocable, knowledge that one acquires all of a sudden when confronted with somebody one loves who is dying, somebody . . .

"You mustn't get excited," she said.

"I'm not excited, I'm just a little restless. Excitement is over as far as I'm concerned."

He had adopted a playful tone. But after all, I'm going to die, he thought, perhaps I ought to talk to her seriously? But what about? About us? But there's nothing left to talk about, or hardly anything. Nevertheless, the mere thought that he could still exert some influence by his words brought back his old impatience.

"I'll do my best," he said. "I'm sorry."

And he reached for her hand with a calm, deliberate gesture. The last time had been two years ago, in the Bois de Boulogne: he was sitting on a bench with a young and rather silly girl and he had made the same calm gesture in order not to alarm her. Pointlessly, as it turned out, for she was back at his flat with him an hour later. But he remembered the immense length of time it had taken before his hand reached those slightly reddened fingers.... It was moments like those ...

"You have nice hands," he said.

She didn't reply. He could hardly see her. He would have liked her to open the shutters, but it occurred to him that darkness was more appropriate to this final act of the play. Play? What gave him that idea? There was nothing theatrical about his situation. But he was doing his best to remedy that.

"It's Thursday today," he said plaintively, "half-holiday. When I was a small boy, I always hoped that a week with four Thursdays in a row would turn up one day.* I still do: then I'd have three days longer to live."

"Don't talk nonsense," she staid with an impatient shrug.

"Oh, no you don't!" he said, suddenly furious, trying to raise himself on his elbows. "You're not going to do me out of my death! You know perfectly well that I'm going to die."

She looked at him with a slight smile.

"Why are you smiling?" he asked in a gentle voice.

"That reminded me of a remark you made—you probably won't remember it—about fifteen years ago. We were at

---

* *Thursday is a half-holiday in French state schools. (Trans.)*

the Faltoneys'. I didn't know that you were being unfaithful
to me at the time, or at any rate I had only a faint
suspicion. . . ."

He felt the stirrings of an old complacency that he
quickly suppressed. What extraordinary situations he had
got himself into, what unbelievable adventures he had had!

"Well, go on."

"That evening I realized that you were Nicole Faltoney's
lover. Her husband wasn't there, and when you brought
me home, you said you had to drop in at your office to
finish something or other. . . ."

She spoke slowly, pausing after every other word. His
thoughts had turned to Nicole. She was blonde, gentle, a
little querulous.

"So then I said I'd like you to come home with me, that
I'd prefer it if you did. I didn't dare tell you that I knew:
you were always talking about the stupidity of jealous
women, and I was afraid . . ."

She spoke more and more softly, dreamily, almost like
someone tenderly recalling an unhappy childhood. It got
on his nerves.

"You mean, I told you I was going to die?"

"No, but you used much the same formula: you said . . .
Oh, no!" she said, and she burst out laughing. "It's too
preposterous . . ."

He began to laugh, too, but halfheartedly. It scarcely seemed the moment for laughter, especially not for her—only he could be allowed such heroic gaiety.

"Well? Go on."

"You said: 'You're not going to deprive me of that woman, you know perfectly well that I want her.' "

"Oh," he said. (He was disappointed, having vaguely expected some witticism.) "There's nothing very funny about that."

"No," she said. "But to say that to me, as though it were self-evident! . . ."

She laughed again, but with a touch of constraint, as though she sensed that he was annoyed.

But now he was busy listening to his heart. Its beat was muffled, pitifully faint. How frail we are, he thought with a touch of bitterness. He was tired of seeing clichés he had despised at the age of twenty being borne out time and again. Death was going to resemble death just as much as love resembled love.

"Ah, well," he said, closing his eyes, "it's been a very accommodating heart."

"What?" she said.

He looked at her. It was strange to be leaving behind one a person primed with such anecdotes, stories against one, against what would be one's ghost. Someone who had been so gentle at twenty, so defenseless, and whom he now

found so changed—whom he would never find again.
Marthe . . . Whatever had become of her?"

"Do you love this man Jean?" he asked.

She answered him, but he wasn't listening. He was
trying once more to count the sunbeams on the ceiling.
The wavering, feathery reflections of the sun. Would the
Mediterranean still be as blue, afterward? Someone was
singing in the courtyard. He had loved a handful of songs
in his life so passionately that, in the end, he could no
longer bear to listen to music. Marthe, on the other hand,
used to play the piano. But good-looking pianos were hard
to find, and he had been very particular when it came to
furniture. So they hadn't had a piano.

"Don't you play the piano any longer?" he asked
plaintively.

"The piano?" she said wonderingly.

She was surprised; she herself couldn't remember
anymore: she had forgotten her youth. He alone retained
the fond memory of Marthe's blonde hair and straight
young neck against the black background of the piano. He
turned his head away.

"Why do you ask me about the piano?" she asked again.

He didn't reply, but he squeezed her hand. His heart
frightened him; he recognized the old pain. He longed for
a moment's reassurance, the comfort of Daphne's
shoulder, the taste of alcohol.

But Daphne was living with that young idiot Guy, and alcohol would only hasten the end. He was afraid, that was all, simply afraid. . . . It was that blankness in his head and that shrinking of his muscles. It was horrible. The thought of his death filled him with such horror that it made him smile.

"I'm afraid," he said to Marthe.

Then he repeated the words, stressing each syllable. They were harsh, rough words, manly words. All the words in his life had been so easy to say, tripping off the tongue: "my darling, my sweet, whenever you like, soon, tomorrow." Marthe wasn't a very soft name and it hadn't come often to his lips.

"Don't worry," she said.

Then she leaned over him and put her hand over his eyes.

"Everything will be all right. I shall be here, I won't leave you."

"Oh, it doesn't matter," he said, "if you have to go out, if you've some shopping to do . . ."

"Later."

Her eyes were full of tears. Poor Marthe, crying didn't suit her. Nevertheless, he felt a little comforted.

"You don't feel bitter toward me?" he said.

"I remember other things, too," she said, dropping her voice to a whisper that reminded him of a dozen similar slightly breathless voices in the corner of a drawing room

or on a beach. His coffin would be followed by a long trail
of whispers, tender and silly. Sitting at home in her
armchair, Daphne, the last of his mistresses, would evoke
his memory, much to Guy's irritation.

"All is well," he said. "I should have liked to die in a
wheatfield, though."

"What do you mean?"

"With the wheat waving over my head. You know the
line: 'the wind is rising, life must go on.' "*

"Calm yourself."

"The dying are always told to keep calm. A fine time to
tell one."

"Yes," she said, "it's the right time."

He thought what a beautiful voice she had. He was still
holding her hand in his. He would die with a woman's
hand in his; all would be well. What did it matter if the
woman was his own wife?

"Happiness between two people," he said, "it's not so
easy."

Then he burst out laughing, because, in the last resort,
he didn't give a damn about happiness. Happiness, or
Marthe, or Daphne. He was nothing but a heart still
beating away, and that, for the moment, was the only
thing that mattered to him.

* *From* "Le Cimetière Marin" *by Paul Valéry. (Trans.)*

The Unknown Visitor

SHE TOOK THE CORNER AT FULL SPEED AND PULLED
up sharply in front of the house. She always sounded her
horn on arrival. She didn't know why, but every time she
arrived home she would give David, her husband, this
warning that she was back. That day, she found herself
wondering how and why she had acquired the habit. After
all, they had been married for ten years, they had been
living for ten years in this charming cottage outside
Reading, and it hardly seemed necessary to announce
herself in this way to the father of her two children, her
husband and ultimate protector.

"Where can he have gone?" she said in the ensuing
silence, and she got out of the car and walked with her

golfer's stride toward the house, followed by the faithful Linda.

Life had not been kind to Linda Forthman. At the age of thirty-two, after an unhappy divorce, she had remained alone—often courted, but still alone—and it required all Millicent's good nature and enthusiasm to endure, for example, this entire Sunday in her company, playing golf. Though uncomplaining, Linda was infuriatingly apathetic. She looked at men (unmarried men, of course), they looked back at her and things never seemed to go any further. To a woman like Millicent, who was freckled and full of charm and vitality, Linda Forthman's character was an enigma. From time to time, with his usual cynicism, David would offer an explanation: "She's waiting for a chap," he would say. "Like every other girl, she's waiting for some chap she can get her hooks into." Not only was it untrue, it was grossly unfair. In Millicent's view, Linda was simply waiting for someone who would love her, for all her apathy, and take her in hand.

Come to think of it, David was very contemptuous and harsh on the subject of Linda, and indeed of the majority of their friends. She must talk to him about it. For instance, he refused to see the good side of that buffoon Jack Harris, who, even if he was as dumb as an ox, was generosity and kindness itself. David was always saying of him: "Jack's a ladies' man . . . without the ladies," at which

point he would roar with laughter at his own joke as
though it were one of the inimitable witticisms of Shaw
or Wilde.

She pushed open the door into the drawing room and
paused, flabbergasted, on the threshold. There were
overflowing ashtrays and opened bottles all over the place
and two dressing gowns lying in a corner in a heap: hers
and David's. For one panic-stricken moment she wanted to
turn around and leave, and pretend not to have seen. She
cursed herself for not having telephoned beforehand to say
she was coming back earlier than expected: Sunday night
instead of Monday morning. But Linda was there behind
her, wide-eyed, a look of dismay on her pale face, and she
would have to think up some plausible explanation for the
irreparable occurrence that had evidently taken place in
her house. Her house . . . ? Their house . . . ? For the past
ten years, she had said "our house" and David "the house."
For the past ten years, she had talked about potted plants,
gardenias, verandas and lawns, and for the past ten years
David had said nothing in reply.

"What on earth," said Linda, and her high-pitched voice
made Millicent shudder, "what on earth has been going on
here? Has David been giving parties in your absence?"

Millicent laughed. She, at least, seemed to be taking it
fairly lightly. And indeed it was perfectly possible that
David, who had left for Liverpool two days before, had

come back unexpectedly, spent the night here and gone out to dine at the nearby country club. Only there were those two dressing gowns, those two gaudy shrouds, those two banners, as it were, of adultery. She was astonished by her own astonishment. After all, David was a very attractive man. He had blue eyes, black hair, fine features and considerable wit. And yet it had never occurred to her, she had never had the slightest presentiment, let alone proof, that he was interested in any other woman. Of that much, without knowing quite why, she was certain. In fact she was absolutely convinced that David had never even looked at another woman.

She pulled herself together, crossed the room, picked up the two incriminating dressing gowns and threw them into the kitchen—hurriedly, but not hurriedly enough to avoid seeing the two used cups on the table and a butter-smeared plate. She shut the door hastily, as though she had witnessed a rape; and, emptying the ashtrays, tidying away the bottles, chatting amiably, she set about trying to distract Linda from her initial curiosity and got her to sit down.

"Such a bore," she said. "Probably the maid didn't come to clean up after last weekend. Do sit down, darling. Shall I make you a cup of tea?"

Linda sat down gloomily, her hand between her knees and her bag dangling from her fingertips.

"If you don't mind," she said, "I'd prefer something stronger than tea. That last round of golf exhausted me. . . ."

Millicent went back to the kitchen, averting her eyes from the cups, grabbed some ice cubes and a bottle of whiskey and set them down in front of Linda. They sat facing each other in the drawing room, that charming drawing room furnished in bamboo and shadowed cretonne, which David had brought back from somewhere or other. The room now looked—if not human—at least presentable once again, and through the French windows the elm trees could be seen swaying in the wind, that same wind that had driven them off the golf course an hour ago.

"David's in Liverpool," said Millicent, and she realized that her voice was peremptory, as though she felt poor Linda was liable to contradict her.

"I know," said Linda amiably, "you told me."

They both stared out of the window, then at their feet, then at one another.

Something was beginning to take hold in Millicent's mind. Like a wolf, or a fox—at any rate, some sort of wild animal—it was gnawing at her. And the pain was getting worse. She gulped down some whiskey to calm herself and caught Linda's eye again. Well, she thought to herself, if it's what I think it is, if it's what any reasonable person might be expected to think it is, at least it isn't Linda.

We've been together all weekend and she's just as appalled as I am, in fact even more so, oddly enough. For, to her mind, the idea of David bringing a woman back to their house, whether or not the children were there, the idea of David bringing that woman here and lending her her dressing gown, still seemed absolutely unthinkable. David never looked at other women. In fact David never looked at anyone. And the word "anyone" suddenly resounded in her head like a gong. It was true that he never looked at anyone. Not even at her. David had been born handsome and blind.

Of course it was natural enough, only seemly, really, that after ten years their physical relations should have dwindled to practically nothing. Of course it was only to be expected that after all this time nothing much should remain of the eager, hot-blooded, highly strung young man she had once known, but even so, it was really rather odd that this handsome husband of hers, so blind but so attractive . . .

"Millicent," said Linda, "what do you make of all this?"

She gestured vaguely around the room, indicating the general disorder.

"What do you expect me to make of it?" said Millicent. "Either Mrs. Briggs, the charwoman, didn't come in last Monday to clean up, or else David spent the weekend here with a call girl."

And she laughed. If anything, she felt rather relieved. Those were the two alternatives; there was no great mystery about it. There was nothing wrong with having a good laugh with a girl friend about being deceived by one's husband and discovering it by chance because it was too windy to play golf.

"But," said Linda (and she, too, was laughing), "but what do you mean, a call girl? David spends his entire time with you and the children and your friends. I can't see how he would have the time for call girls."

"Oh, well," said Millicent, laughing even louder—she really did feel relieved, without knowing why—"perhaps it's Pamela or Esther or Janie . . . Search me."

"I don't think any of them would appeal to him," said Linda, almost regretfully, and she made a move as if to get up, to Millicent's alarm.

"Look, Linda," she said, "even if we had caught them in the act, you know very well we wouldn't have made a scene. After all, we've been married for ten years, David and I. Both of us have had the odd fling . . . there's nothing to make a fuss about. . . ."

"I know," said Linda, "these things don't matter very much. All the same, I must go, I want to get back to London."

"You don't like David much, do you?"

For a second there was a look of amazement in Linda's

eyes, which quickly changed to one of warmth and tenderness.

"Yes, I do, I like him very much. I've known him since I was five years old, he was my brother's best friend at Eton. . . ."

And, having made that pointless and uninteresting statement, she looked intently at Millicent, as though she had just said something of the utmost importance.

"Good," said Millicent. "In that case, I don't see why you can't forgive David for something I myself am prepared to forgive. I know the house is in a mess, but I'd rather stay here than be stuck in that hellish bottleneck all the way back to London!"

Linda picked up the whiskey bottle and poured herself an enormous glassful, or so it looked to Millicent.

"David is very good to you," she said.

"Of course he is," said Millicent unhesitatingly.

And it was true that he had been a considerate husband, courteous, protective and on occasion highly imaginative. He could also, alas, be exceedingly neurotic. But she would keep that to herself. She wasn't going to tell Linda about David lying on the sofa in London with his eyes closed for days on end, refusing to go out. She wasn't going to tell her about David's terrifying nightmares. She wasn't going to tell her about David's manic telephone conversations with some businessman whose name she couldn't even remember. She wasn't going to tell her about David's rages when one of the children failed an exam. Nor would she tell Linda how insufferable David could be about furniture or pictures, nor how forgetful David, the considerate David, sometimes was about his appointments, including those with her. Nor about the state he was sometimes in when he came home. Least of all could she tell Linda about the marks she had seen on his back one day when she caught sight of it in the mirror. . . . And the mere memory of this was enough to break down her conventional English reticence, and she asked—at least she heard herself ask—"Do you really think it's Esther or Pamela?" Because it was true that he didn't have the time to see other women but those. Women, even women who indulge in illicit affairs, demand a certain amount of time from their lovers. David's adventures, if they existed, could only be crude, frantic, hurried affairs, with prostitutes or specialists. And it was surely impossible to imagine David, proud, fastidious David, as a masochist. . . .

Linda's voice seemed to come from a long way away.

"What makes you think of Pamela or Esther? They're much too demanding. . . ."

"You're right," said Millicent.

She stood up, went over to the mirror on the wall and examined herself in it. She was still beautiful—men had told her so often enough, and sometimes proved they meant it—and her husband was one of the most charming and gifted men in their circle. Why, then, did she seem to see in the mirror a sort of skeleton without flesh or nerves or blood or sinews?

"It seems a pity," she said (she hardly knew what she was saying any longer), "it seems a pity that David hasn't more men friends, as well as women friends. Have you noticed?"

"I've never noticed anything," said Linda, or rather Linda's voice, since dusk had descended and all Millicent could see of her was a silhouette, a sort of mouselike creature perched on the sofa who knew—but what did she know? The woman's name. Why didn't she tell her? Linda was nasty enough or nice enough—how could one tell in such cases?—to murmur a name. Why then, in this July twilight, wrapped in her solitude and her pale suit, did she look as though she was scared out of her wits? One must be rational and down-to-earth about these things. If it was true, she would have to face up to the fact that David was having an affair with some woman, either a friend or a professional. Vulgar recriminations must be avoided at all costs, and, perhaps, later on she might even take a lighthearted revenge with Percy or someone. One must see things in their proper perspective, like a woman of the world. She got to her feet, straightened the cushions with a regal hand and declared:

"Listen, darling, whatever happens, we'll stay here the night. I'll go and see what sort of state the rooms are in upstairs. If by any chance my dear husband has been having an orgy, I'll telephone Mrs. Briggs, who lives down the road, and ask her to give us a hand. Does that suit you?"

"Fine," said Linda from the shadows. "Fine. Anything you say."

And Millicent walked toward the staircase, giving the photograph of their sons an absentminded smile on the way. They were to go to Eton, like David, and who else was it? Oh, yes, Linda's brother. Climbing the stairs, she was surprised to find that she needed to lean on the banisters. Something had deprived her of the use of her legs; it wasn't the golf, nor the thought of possible adultery. Anyone can envisage, indeed must envisage, the possibility of one's partner's infidelity—it wasn't an excuse for creating a scene or putting on an act. Not to Millicent's way of thinking, at any rate. She went into "their" bedroom, the bedroom of "their" house, and noticed without the slightest embarrassment that the bed was unmade, the sheets rumpled, churned up as they had never been, it seemed to her, since her marriage to David. Then she noticed the watch on the bedside table, *her* bedside table. It was a heavy waterproof watch, a man's watch, and she weighed it in her hand for a moment, fascinated and incredulous, until the realization that it must have been left behind by another man finally sank in. She understood everything now. Downstairs, there was Linda, worried sick and getting more and more scared, sitting there in the dark. Millicent went downstairs again, and with a curious, almost pitying expression in her eyes, looked at dear Linda, who also knew.

"Linda, my poor pet," she said, "I'm afraid you were right. There's a pair of salmon-pink shorts in the bedroom I wouldn't be seen dead in."

The Five Diversions

IF ONE HAD TO SUM UP THE LIFE OF COUNTESS JOSEPHA
von Krafenberg, famous for her beauty and her natural
cold-bloodedness, one could do so in five "diversions." At
certain crucial moments of her existence, Josepha seems to
have had the surprising knack of detaching herself
completely from the immediate crisis and concentrating
on an apparently insignificant detail that offered a means
of escape.

The first occasion was during the Spanish Civil War, in
a country inn where her young husband lay mortally
wounded. He had called her to his bedside and told her in
a voice which grew gradually weaker that it was thanks to
her that he had first of all enlisted and then deliberately

set out to get himself killed. He told her that her indifference, her coldness in response to his grand passion, had inevitably led to this, and that he hoped that she would one day acquire some of the milk of human kindness. Motionless, immaculately dressed, in that room full of ragged, wounded soldiers, she heard him out. Her eyes roamed about the room with a mixture of curiosity and disgust, and suddenly, through the window, she caught sight of a field of wheat waving in the summer breeze exactly like a landscape by Van Gogh. Extricating her hand from her husband's, she got up, murmuring: "Do look at that field, it's just like a Van Gogh," and stood leaning out of the window for some minutes. Her husband meanwhile closed his eyes, and when she returned to his bedside, to her utter amazement he was dead.

Her second husband, Count von Krafenberg, was a very rich and powerful man who had long dreamed of showing her off as an elegant, intelligent and decorative appendage. They went to the races, made the rounds of the famous Krafenberg stables, lost a quantity of Krafenberg marks at the casino and immersed their bronzed Krafenberg bodies at Cannes and Monte Carlo. Nevertheless, Josepha's coldness, which, of all her qualities, had been the one that most attracted Arnold von Krafenberg in the first place, ended by frightening him. One evening, in their sumptuous apartment on the Wilhelmstrasse, Arnold reproached her for this coldness and even went so far as to ask her if it ever occurred to her to think of anything but herself. "You have refused to give me any children," he told her, "you scarcely open your mouth and, as far as I am aware, you don't even have any friends." She replied that she had always been like that and that he should have known it when he married her. "I have some news for you," he went on coldly. "I am ruined, completely ruined, and we shall have to leave in a month to live quietly in our country house in the Black Forest, which is all I've been able to save." She laughed in his face and told him that he could go without her. Her first husband had left her enough money to live comfortably in Munich and the Black Forest had always bored her to tears. This was too much for the iron control of the celebrated banker, who set about kicking the drawing-room furniture to pieces and shouting that she had only married him for his money, that he had always suspected it and now she had proved it by falling into the trap he had just set her, for he was no more ruined than Onassis was. . . . While he ranted and raved and the precious objects flew through the air, Josepha saw to her horror that she had a run in her right stocking. For the first time since the beginning of this painful discussion she showed some animation and sprang to her feet. "I have a run in my stocking," she said, and to the utter amazement of poor Count Arnold von Krafenberg, left the room.

The Count forgot, or pretended to forget, the incident.
She insisted on having an apartment of her own in the
future, completely separate from his, an apartment with a
large terrace overlooking the whole of Munich, where she
spent her time lying on a chaise-longue in the sun
all summer long, fanned by two enormous Brazilian
housemaids while she stared up at the sky in silence. Her
sole communication with her husband consisted of a
check that was brought to her each month by his private
secretary, a handsome young man called Wilfrid. Wilfrid
quickly fell in love with her, with her apparent tranquility,
and one day, taking advantage of the fact that the two
Brazilians spoke hardly any German, ventured to tell her
that he loved her to distraction. He half expected her to
send him packing and to lose him his job with the Count,
but she had been living on her own, on her terrace, quite
long enough, and she merely said: "Very well . . . I like
you . . . I'm bored. . . ." Then she put an arm around his
neck and, to his intense embarrassment, kissed him
violently under the impassive gaze of the two Brazilians.
When he raised his head, utterly bewildered and overjoyed,
he asked her if and when he might become her lover. Just
at that moment, a feather detached itself from one of the
maids' fans and floated back and forth against the sky. She
followed it with her eyes. "Look at that feather," she said.
"Do you think it will get over the wall, or not?" He looked

at her, dumbfounded. "I asked you when you would give yourself to me," he said with a hint of anger. She smiled and replied, "Here and now," and pulled him toward her. The two Brazilian maids went on waving their fans, crooning softly to themselves.

From behind the desk in his consulting room Dr. Lichter looked at her with a mixture of curiosity and horror. She was as impassive as ever. "I haven't seen you since that poor boy committed suicide," he said, "your husband's secretary." "Oh, Wilfrid," she said. "Did you ever discover why he should have done such a thing in your house?" Their eyes met. The doctor's were contemptuous and challenging, but Josepha's were perfectly placid. "No," she replied, "but I thought it was most uncalled-for."

The doctor winced slightly and opened a drawer, from which he produced several X-ray photographs. "I have bad news for you," he said. "I've already explained the situation to Count von Krafenberg, who asked me to show you these." She pushed the X rays aside with a gloved hand and smiled. "I've never been able to read an X ray. I take it that you have received the result of the tests. Are they positive?" "Alas, yes," he said. They stared at each other, then something caught her eye above the doctor's head and she stood up; she took three steps forward, straightened a picture on the wall and quietly resumed her seat. "Forgive me," she said, "but it was getting on my nerves." The doctor had lost a bet he had made with himself: that for once he would succeed in disconcerting Josepha von Krafenberg.

Josepha was in a hotel bedroom finishing a note to her husband: "My dear Arnold, as you have often pointed out to me, I don't know what it is to suffer. I have no wish to begin now." Then she got to her feet and, calm and pensive as ever, gave herself a final glance in the mirror. Incredibly, she even gave herself a little smile, then walked over to the bed, lay down and opened her handbag. She took out a small black pistol, immaculately polished, and loaded it. Unfortunately, as the mechanism was a little stiff, she broke a nail. Josepha von Krafenberg could not tolerate slovenliness in any circumstances whatsoever. She got up, opened the manicure set she carried with her and carefully repaired the damage. That done, she rearranged herself on the bed and took up the pistol once more. She pressed it against her temple. The shot made hardly a sound.

The Gentlemanly Tree

AT THE TOP OF THE BROAD FLIGHT OF STEPS LEADING
down from the terrace, Lord Stephen Kimberly turned and
held out his hand to his fiancée. In the slanting sunlight of
this fine English autumn evening, she looked even lovelier,
more feminine, more graceful, than usual. He felt a
momentary pang of regret that it all left him completely
cold; but after all, she loved him, or thought she did, she
came from the same background, she had a good dowry
and it was time for him, at thirty-five, to get married. They
would people the English countryside with fine healthy
children who would have their mother's blue eyes and their
father's brown hair, or, conversely, brown eyes and fair

hair. They would utter piercing cries, ride ponies, and be sure to find an ancient gardener to befriend them.

Cynical though Stephen's unspoken thoughts might seem, he was not, in fact, much given to cynicism. Brought up in this house, then at Eton, then in London, he had passed his childhood, his adolescence and his semimaturity in a state of imperturbable calm, except for one episode, of which, at this moment, he had no recollection whatever. Nostalgia lay somewhere at the end of the avenue.

"How gorgeous those beeches are!" cried the lovely Emily Highlife, his fiancée, letting a silvery laugh escape her lips. She herself envisaged with no little pleasure the idea of becoming, one day soon, the mistress of this place, of this man and of the well-bred babies he would duly provide her with. And so, placing her hand on her cavalier's muscular arm, she descended the steps as though treading on air.

Seated beneath a huge parasol, stuffing themselves with tea and scones, their two mothers, both long widowed (one, thanks to the Indies; the other, to the stock exchange), contemplated the pair with intense gratification. The thought of the grandchildren who would undoubtedly be inflicted upon them for a month here, a month there, during the holidays, cast a faint shadow over this golden future, but still . . . there would always be a nanny to cope with them.

"I'm so happy," said Lady Kimberly. "It was high time

Stephen settled down. I didn't much care for his London friends."

"All young people must sow their wild oats," replied the other indulgently. "It will have been all to the good for my little Emily."

While their mothers exchanged these shrewd prognostications, the two young people wandered off down the avenue. Although he often came to Dunhill Castle, Stephen seldom explored the grounds these days. Like many people of his age, he saw little point in moving around unless perched on a vehicle with four wheels or four legs. However, since his fiancée kept going into raptures over those confounded beeches, he strolled listlessly in her wake, looking with unseeing eyes at the sudden oblique descent of the sun through the foliage. And so, without his being aware of it, he came upon the glade again, with her at his side. It was no more than a sort of clearing at the end of the long avenue, very silent and very green, approached by a path overgrown with brambles. And it was there, on seeing the tree again, that he remembered the past, Faye's face and what was possibly the one and only living moment of his life.

He was fifteen years old and she fourteen. She was the daughter of the tenant farmer. She lived a little way off, nearer the river. She was brown-haired and brown-skinned, with that air of some creature of the wild so often found among girls who grow up alone in the country. As for him, he was a gangling, awkward youth dressed in white flannels, for it was diabolically hot that summer at Dunhill. They had begun by tickling the almost tame brown trout of the estate (almost tame but strictly forbidden), and, holding them in his hand, feeling their ice-cold bodies frenziedly quivering in his palm, Stephen had a curious sensation of pleasure, of something forbidden and, even more confusedly, the desire for a different prey, equally frenzied but less icy to the touch. Faye laughed at him, laughed at his accent, his pimples, his awkwardness. She always won their wild games. She was the complete "Unknown," nature and woman personified; she was everything he was ignorant of and had few opportunities of finding out about. But for that one summer, for the first and last time in his life, Stephen succumbed to Dunhill's spell and appreciated its beauties, simply because Dunhill was covered with leaves to lie on, filled with hay to hide in, and because this venerable glade had suddenly become, in the torrid summer heat, a place of illicit delights.

What had to happen happened at the end of a long afternoon. Before kissing him, Faye had said his name, "Stephen," and in that instant he felt as though he were hearing his own name for the first time. Both of them perfectly carefree because perfectly aware that this summer would be the last: she already cynical because already resigned, he practically stupefied with pleasure, neither of them showed for a moment the slightest trace of sentimentality. The summer passed. Thanks to the sun and Faye's expert caresses, Stephen's pimples disappeared, his awkwardness turned to strength and his lies became second nature. Surrounded, hemmed in, by gamekeepers, parents, cousins, huntsmen and other denizens of the locality, Stephen and Faye met every day in the same clearing beneath the same tree: a plane tree that one of his uncles, an eccentric alcoholic Irishman, had brought back from Provence for some unexplained reason and which had been exiled to this glade as though it were the obscure symbol of a hereditary taint. Thus, every afternoon they would rediscover each other's bodies amid the mingled scents of grass and of love. They parted without a word.

When Stephen returned two years later, after the rich young Englishman's traditional sojourn in Europe, he caught a glimpse of Faye while out for a walk, pregnant and indeed happily married. It cannot be said that so much as a glance passed between them. They might have been two dumb animals passing each other by, for all that they could claim to have suffered from their separation. Nevertheless, although their romance had been without poetry and without consequence, one day, when their passion had been more violent than usual, Stephen had carved their initials, "S" and "F," into the bark of the famous plane tree, not with a heart in the middle, but just the two initials "S" "F." And now, on this evening of his engagement, at the sudden thought of those two letters clinging side by side like two leeches, devouring the tree, at the mere recollection of those interminable family dinners that summer, with his trembling hands, his white collar, and deeply disturbing visions flickering before his exhausted eyes, now, at the age of thirty-five, his heart—literally deadened and destroyed by the life he had led since then, by his beautiful fiancée and his ineluctable destiny—began to beat faster. He saw himself again at fifteen, a naked Red Indian in the arms of a black-haired squaw, and he looked at Emily's blonde curls with an almost sexual hatred.

She'll see those initials, he thought. There aren't many names beginning with an "S" in our family, and I'm going to have to explain that frenzied passion to her in terms of some romantic love story. I'll even have to think up a childhood sweetheart. . . .

And even as he racked his brains for some little girl among the neighboring families whose name began with an "F" and whom he might have brought to this place plausibly, during a tea party, or at any rate dressed in some insurmountable crinoline, something inside him balked at this final lie. To be sure, he would be unfaithful to Emily later on, after a decent interval, when they had had their first child, perhaps, and then, of course, he would lie like a trooper. But this was rather different. He hesitated. She turned to him, laughing, and asked him: "But, Stephen, were you expecting me?"

Somewhat taken aback, he stepped up to her side. Her hand was resting on the tree trunk, at the precise spot where the initials were engraved, and, while the "S" was still perfectly legible, the "F" was slightly blurred, the sap having run down the bark and turned the "F" for Faye into something infuriatingly like an "E."

"Stephen-Emily," she said, "even then . . ."

She smiled at him, but Stephen knew that life had just given him, perhaps rather belatedly, a slap in the face from which he would never recover.

An Evening Out

"THERE ARE SOME THINGS ONE CAN ONLY MANAGE to forget by concentrating on other things," she said aloud; and with a short laugh, she stopped pacing up and down her bedroom. There were three possibilities: she could telephone Simon and go out with him; she could take three sleeping pills and sleep until tomorrow (but this futile reprieve did not appeal to her as a solution), or she could try reading a book. But the book would only fall from her hands, no matter how exciting it was, or rather (she could visualize herself exactly), she would put it down on the bedspread and close her eyes, sitting up in bed with the light shining on her eyelids and with this malaise that never left her. Or that left her at certain moments, moments of triumph or gaiety when she told herself, or "admitted" to herself, that she had never loved Marc and that it didn't matter that he had left her. No, a book wasn't the answer: she couldn't bear herself reading, she could only bear herself drowning her sorrows. With "other people."

Telephone Simon. As the number rang out, she moved the receiver from her ear to her cheek and back again, slightly repelled by the black, moist ebonite, hearing the strident tone come and go according to whether or not she held it against her skin. "It would make a good scene in a film," she thought, "the woman telephoning her lover, caressing his voice in advance. . . . Simon's voice was cool; that eternally cool voice of Simon's. She realized that it must be late.

"It's me," she said.

"Are you all right?" asked Simon. "No, you can't be all right if you're telephoning me at this hour."

"Not too bad," she said—and her eyes filled with tears at the tenderness in his voice—"I'm not feeling too bad, but I'd like to go out somewhere for a drink. Are you in bed?"

"No," said Simon, "and what's more, I feel like a drink myself. I'll be round in ten minutes."

No sooner had she hung up and looked at her ravaged face in the mirror, when she felt depressed at the idea of going out, overwhelmed by the desire to stay in this room, by herself, alone with Marc's absence, with what might perhaps properly be termed her grief. Nursing it, giving herself up to it. She was beginning to hate the instinct of self-preservation that had kept her from facing it for the past month, as though it were some kind of bogey. Why not try suffering a little, instead of evading, always evading, everything? Except that it was futile, as futile to give in to unhappiness as it was to try to be happy, as futile as everything else—her life, Simon, this cigarette, which she stubbed out in the ashtray before redoing her face.

Simon rang the doorbell. As they went downstairs together she smiled at him over her shoulder, and he gave her an anxious smile in return. Of course, we were lovers before Marc came along, she thought. I can't really remember exactly how we broke up. In fact, she could remember very little about that period of her life, since everything had crumbled before Marc, tumbling down like the walls of Jericho. She must stop thinking about Marc. She no longer loved him, she didn't want him back; it was herself, really, that she wanted back, herself as she was then, smooth, rounded, fulfilled, revolving in a strange new orbit.

"I'm sick and tired of myself," she said in the car.

"You're the only one who is," said Simon—and he put on a falsetto voice: "We all love you."

"You know, it's like that song by Pierre Mac-Orlan," she said.

"I wish, I wish, if I had the choice,
Never again to hear my own voice . . ."

"Would you like to hear mine?" asked Simon. "I love you, my darling, I love you passionately."

They both laughed. It was probably true. Outside the night club, he put an arm around her shoulders and she leaned against him instinctively.

They danced. The music was wonderfully soothing. She put her cheek on Simon's shoulder, she did not talk. She watched the other couples revolving around her, their faces thrown back in laughter, or alert with expectation, the men's hands pressed to the women's backs, possessively, bodies yielding, to the music's rhythm. Her mind was a blank.

"Such silence," said Simon. "Marc?"

She shook her head.

"There was nothing special about the Marc thing, you know. One mustn't exaggerate these things. Life goes on."

"Luckily," said Simon. "Life goes on, I'm still here, you're still here. We're dancing."

"We'll dance for the rest of our lives," she said. "We're the sort of people who dance."

At dawn they emerged into the fresh air snorting like horses, and Simon's car took them back to his flat. They said nothing, but afterward, on coming back to bed, she kissed him on the cheek and snuggled up against his shoulder, and he put a lighted cigarette between her lips.

Daylight was coming through the curtains, lighting up the clothes on the floor, and she kept her eyes closed.

"You know," she said in a calm voice, "it's funny, just the same—life, all that . . ."

"What?" he said.

"I don't know,"—and turning toward him, she fell asleep on her side. He lay still for a moment, then, having stubbed out both their cigarettes, he, too, fell asleep.

A Stylish Death

SHE WAS BEGINNING TO FEEL BORED, BOTH BY THE place and by her lover. Yet they were the place and the lover of the moment. The "Sniff Club" and Kurt, the handsome Kurt. But although she had always liked such things—handsome men and fashionable night clubs— tonight they were beginning to pall. Once you are past thirty, certain clichés are no longer totally rewarding, especially when they're a bit too loud, like the "Sniff," or a bit too glum, like Kurt. She yawned, and he stared at her closely.

"Are you thinking of Bruno?"

It was a mistake to talk to her about Bruno. Bruno was

her first husband, the only one, the wrench. The man she had lost, had almost gone out of her way to lose, and whose loss she had never been able to accept. He was a long way away now. Nevertheless, she still couldn't bear to hear that name; she, who was supposed to have everything: a vast fortune, two magnificent houses, a lot of charm, a dozen lovers and an unconventional appetite for life.

"Do you mind leaving Bruno out of it. . . ."

"Oh, I beg your pardon! These taboos! Have I annoyed you?"

She turned on him a look of such disarming mildness that he took fright. But too late.

"Have you annoyed me? Yes. I am 'annoyed.' I don't want to see you again, Kurt."

"Do you mean you're kicking me out—as you would your butler?"

"No. I think very highly of my butler."

They looked at each other for a second and he raised his hand to hit her. But she was already on her feet and was now dancing with someone else. He sat staring at his useless hand before sweeping their two glasses off the table and walking out.

Some friends invited her to join them. Much later, she was still dancing. At dawn, she was the last to leave the night club. It was a fresh, blue-tinged dawn like every

dawn that spring. Her car was waiting at the door, a
magnificent brute watched over by a sleepy youth, the
doorman at the "Sniff," who was leaning on the hood in
his page's uniform. Immediately, she felt ashamed.

"I've kept you up very late," she said.

"I'd stay up all night with this beauty."

He couldn't have been more than sixteen or seventeen,
but his admiration was so obvious that it made her laugh.
Just as he was opening the car door for her, a wind
arose, a cool, pungent wind, the first wind of spring. She
felt cold. She was overtired, it was too late, the life she
was leading was idiotic. She looked at the young doorman;
he, too, was shivering slightly in his absurd frogged
uniform. The town seemed empty at that hour.

"Can I drop you somewhere?"

"I live a long way out," he said regretfully, stroking the
car with his hand. "Near Starnberg. I go by train."

She hesitated a moment. Oh, well, why not, a good run
on the highway. And this poor sleepy kid was worn out.
She owed him that much.

"Jump in," she said. "I'm going that way."

"Are you going to your stud farm?"

Ah, yes, the stud farm, the horses at early morning
exercise, the mist in the forest, Bruno . . . She hadn't been
back there since Bruno.

She drove rather too fast through the deserted streets

of Munich. The boy appeared to be in seventh heaven.
He kept glancing delightedly from her profile to the
speedometer and back again.

"It's just near where I live," he said. "That's all I care
about, cars and horses. I wanted to be a jockey, but I'm
already too tall. . . . So I look after the cars at the night
club. How fast can she go?"

They had joined the highway and she would have
preferred to take it easy in her tired state, but something
in her young companion's voice left her no choice. She put
her foot down on the accelerator and the Maserati leaped
forward, whirred, whined, then purred its way up to
120 mph.

"We're doing a hundred and twenty," she said. "How's
that for you?"

He laughed. He looked like nothing on earth with his
uniform and his large, awkward adolescent's hands sticking
out of it. They must have made a comic couple in the
car; she in her evening dress, he in fancy dress. She put
out her hand and switched on the radio. It was the perfect
music, gliding along like the highway beneath her wheels
or beating like the wind at her temples.

"Do you go to your stud farm every morning?"

She hadn't the heart to tell him that she hadn't been
back since Bruno. Not for about two years, in fact. What
must Jimmy be thinking, the old trainer who had taught

her to ride as a child, and who now merely sent her the
bills and those sad, stilted little notes? . . . She had a
sudden desire to see him again. They were almost there
now; it was only twelve miles from Starnberg. . . . She
turned impulsively to the boy at her side:

"Do you want to come to the stud farm with me? You
can watch the first string at exercise, on the gallops. . . ."

"Oh, could I, really?" he said. "If you're sure it's not too
much trouble . . . What a night!"

Well, she thought, at least someone's happy. I haven't
succeeded in making many people happy—not even Bruno,
whom I loved, nor even Kurt, whom I didn't love, nor
any of the others. But this boy is happy. Even for three
hours, that's something.

So they took the turning which led around the lake,
drove through a patch of mist and arrived at the stud farm.
The first person to open the gate was Jimmy, and she
caught a glimpse of his amazed expression. She in evening
dress, the youth in his page's outfit; at six o'clock in the
morning. She got out of the car and fell into his arms.
He had one of those creased good-natured faces typical of
horsey people, an ancient tweed jacket that she remembered
well and a smell of pipe tobacco, which seemed delicious
after the night's cigarettes; unexpectedly so.

"Miss Laura," he said, patting her on the shoulder, "Miss
Laura . . . After all this time . . ."

"Jimmy! It's you . . . Oh, this is . . . uh . . ."

"Gunther," said the little doorman. "Gunther Braun."

He shook hands, his eyes shining. Horses were stamping in their stalls, stableboys forking out hay.

"Come and have some coffee," said Jimmy, leading them into the little office she knew so well. There, on the wall, was a photograph of Laura and Bruno on horseback, and another of Laura, laughing, leaning back to back with Bruno—she recognized the blond head instantly and looked away. And Jimmy did likewise.

"How's the stable doing this season?"

"You must have had my reports. Everything's going fine! Athos was second again in Paris last week, and . . ."

But she wasn't listening. She couldn't tell him that she hadn't read his reports for two years, that she spent her time, with other poor people as rich as herself, shuttling back and forth from Mexico to Capri via the Bahamas. To no purpose. To forget Bruno. And the worst of it was that she was beginning to succeed.

"You must come and watch a gallop," said Jimmy. "There's a colt by Marik! . . . Superb Devil, he's called."

"Like this?"

She indicated her long dress. She was no longer smiling; she was so sleepy she felt ready to drop. . . . The photograph of herself with Bruno was getting on her nerves.

"A gallop? A real gallop?"

Well, all right then . . . The young doorman had waked up and his eyes were shining with excitement. What a night!

"Your things are still upstairs," said Jimmy. "Your jodhpurs and boots . . . That'll do fine, just to go and watch, even if it *is* muddy."

They both gazed at her imploringly. The one aged sixty, the other sixteen, but both with that childish expression that she had always found irresistible in men . . . All right, then, she would go and change, watch one gallop and then go home. Very well. But in the room upstairs, pulling on her boots, she had to pause for a moment, exhausted, her heart thumping, on the verge of nausea. No doubt about it, she was drinking far too much these days. . . .

They took Jimmy's ancient jeep and drove out to where the string was waiting. The horses were snorting, hindquarters steaming, against a background of gray-green trees barely touched by spring. The almost-two-mile track of beaten earth stretched out before them. It all came back to her now: the excitement before mounting, the massed start, the deafening thunder of the gallop and the merciless impact of boot against boot . . . And the ground flying beneath you, and the fear and the fun . . . Ah, yes, it wasn't so long ago that she and Bruno used to do it together.

"I've got a surprise for you," said Jimmy. "Here it is. Jump off, my lad."

Before her stood a superb black horse that she recognized at once. It was Devil, the Marik colt. He was staring at her, and so, too, were all the stable boys and Jimmy and the young doorman.

"I'd like you to try him," said Jimmy. "As you did in the good old days."

She was afraid, horribly afraid. They had no idea what it was like, these people, staying up drinking night after night doing God knows what; they didn't know what it was to feel this exhaustion in the early hours of the morning, to have this trembling in your hands, in your bones. It wasn't fair. She murmured:

"But I haven't been on a horse for two years, Jimmy."

"Never mind, Devil will get you back into the saddle."

He was laughing. Ah, men, sometimes, with their physical strength and their perfect balance . . . And that look in their eyes as well . . . admiration in the boy's, unshakable confidence in Jimmy's. She took a step toward Devil, put a hand on his withers and felt him quiver as though there were already a pact between them. Jimmy cupped his hands and she found herself in the saddle. The beating of her heart made his words almost inaudible:

"Get into line . . . Right . . . Off you go . . ."

And the horses were off, free at last, in the early morning

breeze. She knew at once that it was going to end badly; she passed the first furlong post, then the second, received a clod of earth in the face, felt almost grateful to the earth for this final farewell and then fainted to the apocalyptic sound of thundering hooves, slid gently from the saddle and took Devil's hoof right in the center of her forehead.

The Fishing Expedition

WE WERE IN NORMANDY THAT SPRING, IN MY
sumptuous house, all the more sumptuous for having had
its roof repaired after two years of leaking badly. We
reveled in the sudden absence of basins beneath the beams,
of icy drops on our defenseless sleeping faces at night,
and of squelching carpets underfoot. We decided to
repaint the shutters, which had turned from rust-red to
dirty brown, then brownish gray, and finally, in despair,
had begun to droop lopsidedly at the windows like
banners. This extravagant decision had incalculable con-
sequences of a psychological and sporting nature.

What happened was this:

There was naturally no question of asking an honest-to-goodness local house painter to come along with his cheerful whistling helpers and repaint the dozen or so neglected shutters in a couple of days. Absolutely not. The friend of a friend of ours (when I say "ours," I mean the habitués of the house, who formed an extremely exclusive club—excluding any practical bent, among other things), the friend of a friend of ours, as I say, knew a Yugoslav painter who was extremely intelligent, very gifted, and who did odd jobs to earn his living in France, after numerous political vicissitudes, which need not concern us here. In other words, it was both an economical solution—because everyone knows that local people "take advantage"—and a moral one, since Yasko—which was his name—was rather at loose ends at the moment. Good old Yasko. He was to come with a friend of his who also painted, and his young wife, who would otherwise have been left on her own with nothing to do in Paris. They duly arrived and turned out to be a delightful, talkative trio, much enamored of television: the perfect guests. Without undue haste, the shutters were gradually restored to their former glory.

I don't know why, one fatal day, after three weeks of sustained intellectuality, the conversation should have turned to fishing. Yasko was an angler and had wonderful memories of fishing in his native Yugoslavia. For my part, having caught three sticklebacks in my grandmother's stream when I was ten years old, and later, by some extraordinary chance, after a night of drinking, a sword-fish in the bay of Saint Tropez, I babbled on gaily about harpooning, fly casting and anything else that came into my head. We got quite carried away; Frank Bernard, a writer and good friend who usually confined his observation to Benjamin Constant and Sartre, suddenly discovered a trout from his schooldays. The net result was that the following day found us in a shop that sold fishing tackle, discussing bait, hooks, leads and rods with the utmost seriousness. Later, around the fire, we examined the tide tables. According to Yasko, the best time to go after the fish was just after high tide. There was one at an hour that was out of the question for us, and another just before midday. We decided on the latter, and, for once, we were all in bed by midnight, dreaming of fish.

We had, of course, completely overlooked the fact that Normandy is one of those sensible, quiet places where the few practicable sports are riding, tennis, walks on the promenade and baccarat—if your heart can stand it. If no one of our acquaintance fished, it was for a reason. And if the only people to concern themselves actively with fish were licensed fishermen, those with boats, there was a reason for that, too. One never thinks these things over sufficiently. The fact was, I wanted to impress Madame Marc, our housekeeper, who had sneered at our plans, while Frank was no doubt suffering from a slight Hemingway complex.

So, on the morning in question, in pouring rain, we loaded our fishing rods (light casting) and our earthworms into the car, plus—oh, irony!—a basket for the catch. We had some trouble maneuvering the rods through the windows, and the car looked a bit like a giant pincushion. Frank was still half asleep, the painter and I were in high spirits. The beach was bleak, deserted and freezing cold.

To begin with, we had some difficulty in attaching the worms to the hooks. Frank claimed that his stomach was too delicate for that sort of thing, while I put on the helpless, awkward air of someone who doesn't know the proper way to bait a hook. Yasko had to do it for us. Then he solemnly lifted his arm high and flung his rod. We watched him attentively in order to learn his technique as quickly as possible (I have already explained—I think—that I had but the dimmest memories of the swordfish episode). There was a hissing sound and the hook fell to the ground at Frank's feet. Yasko muttered something about Yugoslav rods—far superior, apparently, to French ones—and raised his arm to cast again. Unfortunately, Frank had helpfully bent down to pick up the hook, and Yasko's upward jerk had the immediate effect of embedding it in the fleshy part of his thumb. Frank gave vent to a string of horrible curses. I jumped to the rescue, removed the hook with its worm from his poor thumb and bandaged it with my handkerchief. That done, for the next five minutes we indulged in a frenzy of activity: whipping the rods back over our heads, trying in vain to get those accursed lines into the water, reeling in at a reckless speed in order to start again, generally acting like three lunatics.

I should add that we had taken our shoes off for this performance and, having carefully rolled up our pants, had left a small pile of our shoes, socks and even watches a few paces behind us. Trusting the tide tables, ignorant as yet of the treachery of the Channel, we paddled along gaily, without a second thought. Frank was the first to see what was happening: his right shoe overtook him, if that's the right word, and was swept out to sea. He gave chase, still swearing, while his left shoe, together with Yasko's socks, bobbed in the surf. There was a moment of indescribable panic: we dropped our rods where we stood, in order to chase after our belongings. The rods were not long in taking to the waves in their turn. And the worms, left to their own devices, floated around with impunity for a good ten minutes, quite long enough to ensure their disappearance for good. We had lost one shoe, two socks, a pair of glasses, a packet of cigarettes and one of the fishing rods. The remaining two were inextricably entangled. It was raining harder than ever. It was exactly twenty-five minutes since we had arrived, triumphantly, on this same beach, and here we were drenched, woebegone, wounded and barefoot. Yasko, as we watched him trying to disentangle his line, looked flustered. Frank sulked on his own, silent and reproachful. Every now and then he sucked his thumb or tried to warm his bare feet between his hands. . . . I tried to salvage the few remaining worms. I was cold.

"I think we've had enough," said Frank suddenly.

He got to his feet and, with a dignity that was all the more praiseworthy as he was limping, walked to the car and slumped down in the back seat. I followed suit. Yasko gathered together the two rods, keeping up a pointless, rambling commentary on the virtues of Yugoslavian shores when it came to fishing and of the Mediterranean when it came to tides. The car smelled of wet dog. The housekeeper made no comment, in itself sufficient indication of the ravages inflicted by our expedition on our normally cheerful faces.

I have never gone fishing in Normandy since. Yasko finished painting the shutters and vanished from our lives. Frank bought a new pair of shoes. We were never destined to be sporting types.

Death in Espadrilles

LUKE HAD HAD A GOOD SHAVE, NOT EVEN CUTTING himself in the process. He was wearing the ultrasmart beige silk suit that his delightful wife, Fanny, had brought back from France, and he was at the wheel of the Pontiac convertible on his way to the Wonder Sisters Studio, whistling in spite of a mild toothache he couldn't quite account for.

It was now ten years since Luke Hammer had started playing the part of Luke Hammer, ten years during which he had been a) a brilliant supporting actor, b) a faithful husband to his French wife, c) a good father to his three children, d) a conscientious taxpayer and, when the occasion arose, e) a good drinking companion. He knew how to swim, drink, dance, apologize, make love, prevaricate, choose, take, accept. He was not quite forty years old and television audiences everywhere had taken him to their hearts. It was therefore with an easy mind that he approached Beverly Hills that morning, choosing his route with precision, on his way to discuss a part that had been recommended to him by his agent and which, in all probability, would be allotted to him by Mike Henry, the boss of Wonder Sisters. His career was in good shape, his life was in good shape and he felt in pretty good shape. At the main intersection on Sunset Boulevard, he hesitated before lighting the mentholated cigarette he allowed himself each morning, so strong was his feeling that the earth and the skies, the sun and the spotlights, were all conspiring to help him to carry on. To carry on providing ketchup and steaks and airplane tickets for the children, the wife, the villa and the garden he had chosen once and for all ten years before (at the same time as he had chosen his name, Luke Hammer). Perhaps a cigarette would trigger off one of those inexorable and terrifying diseases that were the favorite topic in the newspapers in 1975. Perhaps that cigarette would be the last straw that would disclose a hidden weakness unsuspected both by his doctors and himself. This thought surprised him momentarily, for it seemed to him original, and he wasn't accustomed to having original ideas. Despite his prepos-

sessing looks and his well-ordered life, Luke Hammer was
a modest man. So much so that for a long time he had
imagined himself to be riddled with complexes, including
an inferiority complex, until a more than usually stupid,
or crazy, or honest psychiatrist had revealed to him that he
was perfectly normal. The psychiatrist in question was
called Rolland and was, moreover, an alcoholic; remembering this, Luke smiled, and without thinking, threw his
barely touched cigarette out of the car window. What a
pity his wife wasn't there to see him do it. Fanny spent
her entire time telling him to beware of drinking, smoking
and, of course, making love. Love, that is to say physical
love, had been more or less banished from their relations
ever since Luke, or rather Fanny's doctor, had discovered
that he had a slight heart murmur, which, while not
dangerous, could be a handicap, for example in Westerns,
or in those rough-riding films that were, and would
continue to be, his livelihood. At first Luke had taken it
badly, this ban, this sensual and emotional prohibition,
but Fanny had been adamant; she had repeatedly explained
that certainly they had been lovers, and passionate lovers
at that—at which point Luke's brain would be overcome
by a sort of bemused and baffled amnesia—but for the
moment he must learn to forgo certain things and be first
and foremost a father to Tommy, Arthur and Kevin,
who, whether they knew it or not, needed him in order to

live. Needed him with his heart beating regularly, nonstop, day in and day out, like an electronic machine, small, perfect, infallible, punctual, faithful, full stop. His heart being no longer that famished, craving, exhausted, mercurial creature pounding with excitement and panic and pleasure between sheets drenched in sweat, but merely an instrument for recycling his blood, placidly, through equally placid arteries. Placid as the avenues of provincial towns in summer.

She was quite right, of course. And on this particular morning, Luke was especially pleased to be himself, to be able to leap into the saddle at full gallop in front of the cameras, to be able to walk for miles or climb steep slopes, beneath a torrid sun, and even, if he had no objection and because it was the fashion, to be able to simulate an orgasm with a starlet in front of fifty studio technicians as unmoved as himself. Thrilled, in fact.

He was only a few blocks from his destination; a right turn, then a left, and he would arrive in the studio forecourt, hand over the Pontiac to old Jimmy, and, after the usual ritualistic banter, sign the contract drawn up by his agent and good old Henry. True, it was a second lead, but a very good second lead, one of those supporting roles of which he was said to have the secret. A curious phrase, that, when you thought about it: always having the secret of roles that held no secret. He spread out his hand, noticed

with wonder and then with frank admiration how well
manicured, clean, neat, bronzed and virile it was, and
once again was grateful to Fanny. It was thanks to her
that the barber-manicurist had come two days before,
thanks to her that his hair was not too long and his nails
were not too short, that everything was in perfect propor-
tion. Perhaps he was simply short on imagination.

The phrase shattered him. As though some poison, some
dose of LSD or cyanide, had suddenly begun coursing
through his veins: *Short on imagination.* "Am I short on
imagination?" he asked himself. And instinctively, like
someone who had just received a blow, he pulled over to
the side of the road. What did it mean, to be short on
imagination? He knew plenty of intelligent people,
intellectuals even, and writers as well, and they were
proud to know him. And yet that phrase, short on
imagination, seemed to be lodged right between his
eyebrows, and it gave him exactly the same sensation as he
had had twenty years earlier, in the Marines, when he had
surprised his girl friend in the arms of his best friend on
a beach in Honolulu. His jealousy had lodged there, at
exactly the same spot and with the same intensity. He tried
to "see" himself, and out of habit tilted the rearview
mirror and looked at himself. It was him all right: he
looked handsome and masculine, and he was sure that the
tiny broken blood vessel in his eye was merely the result

of a beer or two too many the night before. In the dazzling Los Angeles sunlight, with his pale-blue shirt, his beige, almost white suit, his watered-silk tie and his light tan due partly to the sea air and partly to some marvelous new gadget of Fanny's, he was the living image of health and well-being, and he knew it.

In that case, what was he doing parked like a fool by the sidewalk? In that case, why was he so reluctant to restart the engine? In that case, why was he suddenly sweating, dry-mouthed, scared? And why, all of a sudden, was he having to resist the desire to fling himself down on the car seat, crush his beautifully pressed suit, bite his knuckles? (And bite them until the blood spurted from his mouth, his own blood, so that at least he would have a good reason for the pain he felt. At any rate, a definable reason . . .) He stretched out his hand and switched on the radio. A woman was singing, a negress perhaps. Definitely, in fact, for there was something in her voice that soothed him a little, and he knew from experience that black women, or rather their voices, since he had never, thank God, had any physical contact with them (not out of racism but precisely from lack of racism); anyway, in general, black women's voices, honeyed and raucous, gave him a feeling of moral well-being. And, strangely enough, of solitude. They changed him—not surprisingly, since with Fanny and the children he was anything but a solitary man. But there was also something in those voices that reawakened in him some adolescent feeling, the old mixture, once more, of frustration, insecurity and fear. The woman was singing a half-forgotten, rather old-fashioned song, and he found himself trying to remember the words with an anxiety that verged on panic. Perhaps he ought to pay his alcoholic psychiatrist another visit and, while he was at it, have a thorough check-up—it was over three months since his last one, and Fanny was always saying that one couldn't be too careful. In a job like his, living on your nerves, competition and tension were not just empty words. Yes, he would go and have an electrocardiogram, but in the meantime he must get the car going, get Luke Hammer going, get the new part, his double, himself—he couldn't tell who or which—going. And he must get them all to the studio. It wasn't far now.

"*What are you listening to?*" sang the woman on the radio, "*Who are you looking for?*" and, by God, he couldn't remember what came next. He longed to be able to remember the rest of the song, to get ahead of the singer, so that he could turn off the radio, but his memory refused to click; and yet he knew it was a song he once used to sing, used to know by heart. Still, he wasn't a twelve-year-old anymore, he wasn't the type to stay glued to the curb for the sake of the words of some old blues lyric, not when he had an important appointment and unpunctuality was frowned upon, at least for supporting actors, in the good city of Hollywood.

With what seemed to him to be a colossal effort, he stretched out his hand again to switch off the radio, to "kill" the woman who was singing and who might have been—he told himself in a sort of delirium—who might have been his mother, his wife, his mistress, his daughter. And as he did so, he realized that he was completely drenched: his beautiful beige suit, his shirt cuffs, his hands, were soaked in a sort of horrible sweat. He must be close to death, he thought instantly, and he was surprised to feel no emotion, or even physical pain. The woman was still singing, and against his will he allowed his virile, well-manicured hand to fall back on his knee; and in a sort of painless, peaceful trance he awaited his inevitable death.

"Hey! Hey, there! Gee, I'm terribly sorry . . ."

Someone was trying to tell him something; there was still a human being on this earth who cared what happened to Luke Hammer; but despite his natural courtesy and good humor he couldn't summon the energy to turn his head. He heard footsteps approaching, exceptionally light and soft. How strange: surely death wouldn't come in espadrilles? Suddenly a man's face loomed over him, brick-red, square, with very black hair and a voice that spoke very loud—or so it seemed to him—at any rate loud enough to drown that unknown but familiar voice of the woman on the radio.

At last he took in what the man was saying:

"Sorry, pal, I didn't see you parked there and I had my sprinkler turned on because of the begonias. . . . I guess you must be soaked."

"Forget it," said Luke Hammer—and he closed his eyes for a moment because the man smelled strongly of garlic—"it doesn't matter; in fact it cooled me off. Was it your sprinkler that . . . ?"

"Right," said the man with the garlic breath, "it's a new system, with a mighty powerful engine. I can turn it on from the house. I didn't bother to look; there's never anyone here. . . ."

The man looked at Luke's drenched suit and decided that he must be somebody important. True, he didn't recognize him, but people never recognized Luke right away; it "came back to them" later, when someone said surely that was the fellow in such-and-such a film who played so-and-so. . . . Fanny, in fact, was very good at explaining to people why they only recognized him "later."

"Anyway, I sure am sorry," the man was saying. "But what the hell were you doing here in the first place?"

Luke looked up at him and then looked quickly down again. Without knowing why, he somehow felt ashamed.

"Nothing," he said. "I stopped to light a cigarette. I was

on my way to the studios, you know, the ones just down the block, and, well, it's dangerous to light a cigarette while you're driving, or at any rate it's stupid, I mean . . ."

The man with the garlic breath straightened up and laughed.

"Well, say . . . If that's the worst danger you'll ever have to face, lighting a cigarette or being on the receiving end of a hose, you won't come to much harm! Anyway, sorry again, pal!"

And instead of slapping Luke on the back, he slapped the back of the car and walked off. A sly, bitter, ironical smile came over Luke's face. Just look at me. Here I am, not allowed to do anything anymore, not even make love; here I am, not even capable of dying, but actually capable of believing I'm near death because of some garden sprinkler; here I am, soaked to the skin and hoping to get a minor cowboy role in Hollywood. It's really laughable! But just then, taking a last look at himself in the rearview mirror, he saw that his eyes were full of tears, and he recalled the words of the song that the black woman, or white woman, had been singing. And he knew that he was in excellent health and no mistake.

Five months later, for reasons unknown, Luke Hammer, a hitherto quiet-living actor with Wonder Sisters, succumbed to an overdose of barbiturates in the bedroom of some obscure call girl. No one ever knew why, probably not even the man himself. His wife and three children, it appears, conducted themselves with admirable dignity at the funeral service.

The Left Eyelid

THE MISTRAL—THE TRAIN, NOT THE WIND—WAS
tearing through the countryside. Sitting by one of the
portholelike windows of that closed, blocked-up, almost
hermetically sealed train, Lady Garrett, aged thirty-six,
was musing once again on how much she would have liked
to live in one of those humble or luxurious shacks on the
banks of the Seine between Paris and Melun. A perfectly
understandable sentiment: she had led a hectic life, and
everyone who leads a hectic life dreams of calm, childhood
and rhododendrons, just as those who lead a quiet life
dream of vodka, razzmatazz and wickedness.

Lady Garrett had made a name for herself, so to speak,
in many a scandal and many a love affair. That day,

while admiring the lazy calm of the banks of the Seine, she passed the time by rehearsing what she would say to her lover, Charles Durieux, an auctioneer in Lyon, when she got there: "My dear Charles, it's been a delightful interlude, as uneventful as to be positively exotic, but we must face the fact that we're not really made for each other . . ." At which point Charles, dear Charles, would blush and stammer; she would hold out a regal hand in the bar of the Royal Hotel—giving him no option but to kiss it—and then disappear, leaving behind her lingering looks, whiffs of scent, slow waltzes, memories . . . Poor Charles, dear Charles, so devoted behind his little goatee . . . A fine-looking man, too, and a virile one, but when all was said and done, a provincial auctioneer! He himself ought to have realized that it couldn't last— that she, Letitia Garrett, née Eastwood, whose former husbands included an actor, a sheik, a landowner and a company chairman, could hardly be expected to end her days with an auctioneer! . . . She nodded her head, then quickly stopped herself. She had a horror of those mechanical gestures that people make when alone, at home, in the street, anywhere, in silent corroboration of their private decisions. She knew them only too well, those nods, frowns and chopping gestures with the hand that are characteristic of solitary women—and men who live alone, too—regardless of their mental health or social

class. She took out her powder compact, gave her nose
a perfunctory dab, and once again caught the eye of the
young man two tables away, who had never taken his
eyes off her since they left Paris, thereby reassuring her
that she was still the lovely, mysterious and adorable
Letitia Garrett, newly divorced from Lord Garrett and
handsomely provided for by him.

It was strange, when you came to think of it, how all
those men had loved her so much, who had all been so
proud of her and so jealous, had never, in the end, resented
her deserting them; they had all remained her friends.
She congratulated herself on this, but it may have been
that, at heart, they had all felt a certain relief at no longer
having to share her perpetual state of indecision. . . . As
Arthur Connolly, one of her richest lovers, used to say:
"One could no more leave Letitia than she could leave
you!" He was rich, but he was also a poet, that man. It was
he who used to say of her: "Letitia is all that is evergreen,
tender, girlish," and these three words had never failed
to infuriate the women who succeeded her in Arthur's life.

The menu seemed inexhaustible. She flicked through it
absentmindedly and was faced with the prospect of an
appalling brew consisting of celery rémoulade, a historical
sole (Walewska) and a revolutionary steak (Mirabeau),
plus soufflée potatoes, overripe cheeses and vanilla-flavored
bombes from a packet. It was odd how train menus

nowadays always seemed to be half Michelin, half
Michelet. She smiled at the thought that one of these days
she might come across a *sole guillotinée* or something
equally absurd, and then glanced questioningly at the
elderly lady sitting opposite. She belonged unmistakably
to their destination, Lyon. She looked mild, faintly ill
at ease and utterly respectable. Letitia handed her the
menu and the old lady immediately nodded, smiled and
handed it back with a flurry of amiable and polite gestures
that made Letitia realize the degree to which, despite the
passage of time, she still looked a typical Englishwoman.
"*Après vous,*" said the old lady, "*après vous.*" "*Mais
non, je . . .*" replied Letitia faintly (and, as always on such
occasions, she heard her English accent becoming more
pronounced) . . . "*Mais non. Croyez-vous que le melon
est bon?*" "Soit *bon,*" an interior voice automatically
corrected her, too late. Already, the woman opposite her
was smiling indulgently at her grammatical error, and
she didn't have the courage to correct it herself. She felt
thoroughly disconcerted, then quickly told herself that it
was idiotic to get upset over something so trivial and that
she would do better to think about the little speech she
would be making to Charles in three hours' time. When it
came to addressing a lover, grammar didn't enter into it;
the most you could say—her not inconsiderable knowledge of French had taught her—was that the position of

the words completely altered the meaning of a sentence. For example, between saying to a man "*Je vous aime beaucoup*" and "*Je vous ai beaucoup aimé*" or "*Je vous aimerai toujours*" and "*Je vais toujours vous aimer,*" there were innumerable shades of meaning, which she had the utmost difficulty in sorting out, as much on the sentimental as the grammatical level.

The train was certainly going at a crazy speed. She felt that it would be a gesture of goodwill on her part, of politeness toward the dining car as a whole, if she went and freshened her makeup, washed her hands and combed her hair before the arrival of the flaming steak, the guillotined sole and the unexploded *bombe* which were to constitute her immediate fate for the next hour or so. She gave the woman from Lyon a little smile, and, with her unmistakable walk—somewhat less steady than usual on this train, it had to be admitted—approached the automatic glass doors, which promptly slid apart, pre-cipitating her willy-nilly into the ladies' lavatory on her left. She hastily locked the door. Progress, speed and silence were all very well, but you needed muscles of steel, the agility of a mountain goat and the head of a tightrope walker in order to negotiate a simple compartment between Paris and Lyon these days. She felt a pang of envy for those astronauts who had traveled all the way to the moon and landed on it, seemingly without the slightest jolt, without any cloakroom problems, and returned straight into the sea, straight into the welcoming arms of cheerful sailors. Whereas the welcoming arms awaiting her, at her destination, belonged to a provincial auctioneer, jealous, morose, and with every reason to be so, since, after all, the sole purpose of this hurtling high-speed journey was to break off the relationship.

Here in these antiseptic, dun-colored, grotesque sur-roundings it was even worse than in the compartment, which, with its neat little rep, its neat little carnations and its already outdated modernism, at least made some attempt at comfort. The surfaces of the washbasin were all curved, and, clinging to a tap for support, she tried to open her overstuffed handbag; the train was coming into Dijon and the jolt of the brakes caused the bag, caught between two contrary forces and undecided whether to obey her law or Faraday's, to crack under the strain, break open and spill its contents. She had to get down on all fours and scrabble around, banging her head on the basin and other protuberances in the process, picking up her lipstick here, her compact there, her check book and tickets somewhere else; and by the time she had struggled to her feet, her forehead lightly beaded with sweat, the train had come to a peaceful standstill at Dijon. With a bit of luck, she would have two or three minutes' peace

in which to put on her mascara without having to go
through a Marcel Marceau type of pantomine.

Needless to say, her mascara was the one object that had
not shot out of her bag, and she searched feverishly for
ten seconds before putting her hand on it. She began
with her left eye. As it happened, it was her favorite eye,
the left one. For some unknown reason all her lovers and
all her husbands had preferred her left eye to her right
and had told her so. "It has a more tender expression,"
they would say, and she always amiably agreed that she
looked better on the left side than on the right. It was odd,
really, the way you came to see yourself through other
people's eyes. It was always the men who didn't attract
her in the least who had pointed out the prominence of
the Mound of Venus in her palm, and hence her sensuality.
It was always the men who bored her who had told her
how amusing she was, and, saddest of all, it was always
the men she loved who had told her how selfish she was.

The train started up again with a tremendous jolt, which
sent her reeling and at the same time made her smear her
cheek with a long black trail of mascara. She swore
under her breath in English, and instantly reproached
herself. After all, she was about to meet and break with a
French lover. In her wanderings around the world, Lady
Garrett had acquired the habit of thinking, meditating
and even suffering in the languages of her various lovers.

She therefore substituted for her English oath, out loud this time, another oath of similar meaning but in the purest French, put her mascara back in her bag, and decided that the lady from Lyon would have to put up with the sight of someone with only one eye done. She patted her hair and went to let herself out.

Without success. The door refused to budge. She smiled, rattled the handle, shook the door and had to conclude that something was wrong. It made her laugh. The fastest and most modern train in Europe had a tiny fault in its lock design. After six or seven attempts, it dawned on her that the countryside was still flashing past the little window to her left, that her bag was well and truly fastened, that she herself was all prepared to tackle that wretched menu, but that this door had somehow interposed itself between her and that immediate prospect, uninviting though it was.

She rattled the door again; shook it; banged it, her anger rising like a sort of lava, an absurd, childish anger, the anger of a claustrophobe, except that she didn't suffer from claustrophobia. Thank God, she had always managed to escape such modern neuroses: claustrophobia, nymphomania, mythomania, drug-mania, and so forth. Or so she believed. But now, suddenly, she, Letitia Garrett, who had been taken to the Gare de Lyon by her chauffeur this

fine September morning and was awaited at Lyon itself
by her devoted lover, found herself in the process of
breaking her nails, losing her temper and drumming her
fists on a door made of solidified plastic that refused to
yield to her will. The train had picked up speed again, and
the vibration was such that, the first wave of anger
having subsided, she resigned herself to the worst—in
other words, to waiting—and, modestly lowering the
lid, sat down on the toilet seat, her legs folded beneath
her in a way she would never have sat in a room
full of men, all of a sudden behaving like a prudish
virgin. Perhaps it was because she felt foolish. She saw
herself in the mirror, or rather caught the odd glimpse of
herself, her handbag clutched in her lap as though it
were her most treasured possession, her hair disheveled,
only one eye made up. To her astonishment, she realized
that her heart was thumping wildly, as it had not done for
a long time, not for poor old Charles, who was waiting
for her, nor for poor old Lawrence—the one before—
who, thank God, wasn't waiting for her anymore. Someone was bound to come eventually, and the door would
be opened automatically from the outside. Unfortunately,
all the likely people were having lunch, and the French
never left the table in the middle of a meal, no matter
what happened; they were riveted to their food, to the
procession of waiters, to their precious bottles. Not one

of them would dream of interrupting that unalterable ceremony that was their daily ritual. Once or twice, to pass the time, she pressed the foot pedal that flushed the bowl; then, still sitting in the same ridiculous dignified pose, she decided that she would try to make her right eye match her left one. Thanks to the train's sensational speed, this operation occupied a good ten minutes. By now she needed a drink and was beginning to feel hungry. Tentatively she tried the door again, still in vain. Well then, she must just keep calm and wait until a passenger from one of the adjoining compartments, or the conductor or a waiter or someone, wanted to use the lavatory, and then she would be able to return to her seat opposite the lady from Lyon and prepare her speech for Charles. And anyhow, since she was here, in front of a mirror, why not rehearse it now? She gazed at her large brown eyes and beautiful brown hair in the small and not very flattering mirror provided by French Railways and began:

"Charles, my dear Charles, if I'm saying these cruel things to you now, it's because I'm too fickle, too volatile a person—how shall I put it?—it's something I've suffered from all my life, just as I've made others, besides you, suffer because of it, and I'm too fond of you, Charles, even to contemplate the frightful scenes we would very soon find ourselves having, you and I, if, as you so sweetly suggested, I were to agree to marry you."

Through the porthole to her left the corn shocks lay like golden ninepins at the foot of the green and bronze-colored hills, and she felt her emotions swell with her words:

"After all, Charles, your life is divided between Paris and Lyon and me. Whereas mine is divided between Paris and the rest of the world. You break your journeys at Chambéry, I break mine in New York. We don't live at the same pace. Maybe I've done too much living, Charles," she said. "I'm no longer the young girl you deserve."

And it was true that Charles deserved a girl who was as sweet and trusting as he was himself, and as naïve. It was equally true that she didn't deserve him. Her eyes suddenly filled with tears. She wiped them away impatiently and realized as she did so that she was still sitting there, on her ludicrous perch, with her mascara running, her mouth open, alone. After a short pause, laughter overwhelmed her; she wept with laughter, all alone, without knowing why and without being able to stop, clinging to the special kind of handle provided for the aged and infirm. She saw herself as Queen Elizabeth II before Parliament, or Queen Victoria, or some such personage, making a speech from the throne to an invisible audience, silent and dismayed. Suddenly, she saw the door handle move downward, then up and down again. She sat there petrified with hope, her bag in her hand, ready to jump up and run. Then the handle ceased to move and she realized with horror that someone had come; had thought, with good reason, that the place was occupied, and had quietly gone away again. She must keep an eye on it from now on, and shout. For that matter, why not start shouting now? She didn't want to spend the next two hours in this squalid place. There must be some solution, some passerby would be sure to hear her cries, and, after all, better to look ridiculous than to endure the deadly boredom that, inevitably, would be the next thing. At first, she shouted "Help!" in a rather hoarse voice; then, remembering that she was in France, "*Au secours! Au secours!*" in a screech that, God knows why, sent her into another fit of giggles. To her own amazement, she found herself back on her makeshift seat, holding her sides with laughter. Perhaps, once she had broken with Charles, it might be a good idea to have some sort of psychiatric checkup at the American Hospital or somewhere. . . . Really, it was her own fault; she ought never to travel alone. "They" had always told her: "Don't travel alone." For after all, if Charles had come to fetch her, as he had in fact begged to be allowed to do on the telephone, he would be searching everywhere for her, knocking on every door, and she would have been freed by now and digging into her Sole du Barry, or whatever, under Charles' tender, protective gaze. *If* Charles had been there . . .

But thanks to her own instructions, Charles was probably, in fact certainly, already waiting at the station in Lyon, flowers in hand. He couldn't know that his beloved was trapped like a wild animal within four blank walls, and that he would probably find a disheveled, distraught, nerve-shattered woman by the time her journey was over. No books, even! She didn't even have a book in her bag! The only available reading matter in this place was a notice exhorting her to take care when opening the door, to use the correct exit and not to leave the train unless it was standing at a platform. That was ironic; that was really funny! She would have given anything to get out of this ghastly place, to jump out of the train. Anything rather than this antiseptic box, this humiliating situation, this direct assault on her liberty such as no one had dared attempt for a good ten years, at least. No one, during the past ten years, had dared to keep her within four walls. Not only that, but for the past ten years there had always been a man ready to liberate her from anyone or anything at the drop of a hat. But now she was as alone and abandoned as an unwanted pet, and she gave the door a violent kick that hurt her horribly, spoiled one of her new Saint Laurent shoes and achieved precisely nothing.

Nursing her foot, she sank back onto the seat and caught herself murmuring: "Charles! Oh, Charles!"

Of course, Charles had his faults: he was finicky, and, quite honestly, his mother was no joke, nor were his friends, and, quite honestly, she had known plenty of men who were better company, better-looking and altogether more interesting. All the same, if Charles had been there every door of every cloakroom on every train would have been opened long before this, and he would be gazing at her with those spaniel eyes of his; he would put one of his large hands, so long and at the same time so square, over hers, and say, "Were you very frightened? I hope this stupid business hasn't been too unpleasant for you," and he would even go so far as to apologize for not having done something sooner, and perhaps mutter something about suing the railway company: he was capable of acting quite wildly, despite that calm exterior. In any case, he wouldn't allow anything unpleasant to happen to her. Charles was a man who worried about her well-being, and, when you thought about it, such men were a dying breed. Not that she was short of men to fuss over her— it wasn't that—the notion was too vague and self-evidently absurd, but in general there was a shortage of men who fussed over women. All her friends said the same thing, and when you came down to it they were probably right. It was a well-worn cliché among her generation, but it wasn't so far out. For after all, Lawrence, in the same circumstances, would have assumed, when she didn't reappear, that she had got off at Dijon in order to meet another man, and Arthur would have thought . . . nothing; he would have sat drinking all the way to Lyon, making an occasional inquiry of the chief steward, and in the end only Charles, with his striped tie and his air of calm, would have turned the Mistral upside down to find her. Yes, it was a great pity that they had to part. In fact, come to think of it, it was ridiculous. Here she was, at the age of thirty-six, having done nothing else for twenty years but devote herself to men—her men—their idiosyncrasies, their intrigues, their wives, their ambitions, their disappointments, their desires; and now, on this train, trapped in the most grotesque way imaginable by a recalcitrant door lock, there was suddenly only one man she could think of who could get her out of there, and it was to this very man (thanks to whom she was on this train and toward whom she was hurtling) that she was about to announce once and for all that she had no need of him, nor he of her! And to think that only an hour ago, on getting into the train, she had been so sure of her decision! To think how resolutely she had told her chauffeur, Achille, to come and collect her at the same time tomorrow, by which time she would have thrown off her chains! (This to herself, of course.) And with what joy she had imagined, only that morning, the idea of returning to Paris, alone and independent, with no more lies or commitments; without feeling the slightest obligation to wait in for a telephone call from Lyon, or to refuse an amusing dinner party because of a possible arrival from Lyon, or to cancel an intriguing engagement at the last minute because of the presence of Lyon. . . . Yes, waking up that morning at home, she had felt exultant, suddenly confronted on the one hand with the pleasure of taking the train, for once, through the beautiful French countryside, and on the other, with the more malicious pleasure of being honest and straightforward, and of going all that way in order to demonstrate to someone how honest and straightforward she was, even though lost to him. There had always been a streak of cruelty in her that could easily turn to exultation; but now, this femme fatale foiled by a door lock had become a sort of hideous caricature of herself, and neither her future nor her past seemed to fit into the jigsaw puzzle of her face reflected by the distorting mirror of the train— an optical puzzle that was the product of tears of laughter and exasperation.

After a while there was a constant stream of impatient men, or women—how could she tell?—who came and rattled the door and at whom she yelled "Help!" or

"*Au secours!*" or "Please!" in every tone of voice from a whisper to a shout. Her childhood, her marriages, the children she might have had, the children she had had, all passed through her mind. She remembered silly details, of beaches, whispers in the night, tunes, escapades, and, since she was not devoid of humor, the thought also occurred to her that no psychiatrist's couch could be as effective as a locked lavatory in a first-class carriage between Paris and Lyon.

She was released after Chalon and she didn't even think to tell her rescuer—the lady from Lyon, as it happened— that she had been there for so long. At all events, she got off the train perfectly made-up, perfectly calm, and Charles, who had been waiting anxiously on the platform for nearly an hour, was amazed at how young she looked. He ran toward her, and for the first time since he had known her, she clung to him a little, laid her head on his shoulder and confessed to being tired.

"But it's supposed to be a very comfortable train," he said.

"Yes, I know," she murmured vaguely, and then, turning toward him, she asked him the question that would make him the happiest man in the world:

"And when would you like us to get married?"

A Dog's Night

IN APPEARANCE, M. XIMENESTRE CLOSELY RESEMBLED
a drawing by Chaval: corpulent, with an air of amiable
bewilderment. But now that the month of December had
begun, he wore an expression so woebegone as to make
every passerby with any heart at all want to stop and
ask him what the matter was. The trouble lay in the ap-
proach of Christmas, which M. Ximenestre, good Christian
though he was, was this year contemplating with dismay,
not having a sou with which to pamper the gift-hungry
Mme. Ximenestre, his good-for-nothing son, Charles, and
his daughter, Augusta, an excellent calypso dancer. Not
a sou: that was the exact state of his affairs. And there was
no question of advances or loans. Both had already been

obtained, without the knowledge of Mme. Ximenestre and his children, in order to gratify the latest vice of this supposed breadwinner; in short, to gratify M. Ximenestre's fatal passion: gambling.

Not just the ordinary kind of gambling where the gold trickles over the green baize, nor yet the kind where horses strain to the last gasp over another sort of green baize, but a game, yet unknown in France, which had, alas, become the craze in a café in the XVIIe arrondissement where M. Ximenestre was in the habit of taking a glass of vermouth every evening before going home: a game of darts, but played with a peashooter and ten-franc notes. All the regulars were mad about it, apart from one man, who had had to give it up owing to chronic shortage of breath. Imported by an Australian newly arrived in the district, this thrilling game had quickly become the object of an exclusive club, which met in the back room, where the proprietor, a fan himself, had sacrificed the billiard table.

To cut a long story short, M. Ximenestre had ruined himself, despite a promising start. What was he to do? From whom could he borrow the money for the handbag, the motor scooter and the record player that, from various pointed hints at mealtimes, he knew were expected of him? The days passed, eyes glowed with anticipation and the snow began to fall with gay abandon. M. Ximenestre's

complexion took on a yellowish tinge and he hoped that
he might fall ill. In vain.

On the morning of Christmas Eve, M. Ximenestre left
home followed by three expectant glances, Mme.
Ximenestre's daily search having failed to reveal the
longed-for parcels. He's cutting it fine, she thought, rather
sourly but without a trace of anxiety.

In the street, M. Ximenestre wound his scarf three times
around the lower half of his face, and in doing so,
momentarily contemplated a holdup. An idea he quickly
rejected, fortunately. He padded along in his bearlike
fashion, shambling and good-natured, and ended up on a
bench, where the falling snow soon threatened to turn
him into an iceberg. The idea of the pipe, the briefcase
and the bright-red tie (incidentally unwearable) that he
knew to be awaiting him at home only served to add to
his misery.

There were a few passersby, with glowing cheeks,
springy step and parcels dangling from every finger:
husbands and fathers worthy of the name. A limousine
drew up in front of M. Ximenestre, and a dream creature,
followed by two lapdogs on a leash, got out. M. Ximenestre, albeit an admirer of the fair sex, looked at her without the slightest interest. Then his eyes strayed to the
two dogs and suddenly lit up with a bright gleam. Brush-
ing off the pile of snow that had accumulated on his

knees, he jumped to his feet and uttered an exclamation, which was smothered by the snow that came tumbling from his hat into his eyes and down his neck.

"The dogs' home!" he cried.

The dogs' home was a dismal place, and the inmates, either pathetic or frantic, rather alarmed M. Ximenestre. He finally picked out a dog that was indefinable as to breed and color but had, as they say, nice eyes. And M. Ximenestre was quite sure that it would take the nicest of eyes to make up for a handbag, a record player and a scooter. He christened his find "Rover" without further ado, and leading him on a length of rope, ventured into the street.

Rover's joy found immediate expression in a frenzy that communicated itself willy-nilly to M. Ximenestre, who was taken by surprise at such canine energy. He was dragged along for several hundred feet at a fast trot (the time when the word gallop could be applied to M. Ximenestre was long past) and ended up by barging into a passerby, who grunted something about "dirty brutes!" Like a water-skier, M. Ximenestre thought that his best course might be to let go of the rope and return home. But Rover, barking, jumped up at him with delight, his dirty yellowish coat full of snow, and it crossed M. Ximenestre's mind that it was a long time since anyone had made such a fuss over him. His heart melted. His blue

eyes gazed deep into Rover's brown ones and they shared
a moment of indescribable sweetness.

Rover was the first to recover. He took off again down
the street and the chase continued. M. Ximenestre thought
vaguely of the anemic basset hound that had been in the
kennel next to Rover's, and that he hadn't even considered, being of the opinion that a dog should be robust.
By now he was literally flying in the direction of home.
They stopped in a café just long enough for M. Ximenestre
to gulp down three rums and Rover three lumps of
sugar, which were presented to him by the sympathetic
proprietress. "Poor dog, hasn't he got a little overcoat,
then, in this nasty cold weather!" M. Ximenestre, panting
from his exertions, did not reply.

The sugar had an invigorating effect on Rover, but it
was a pale shadow of a man who rang the doorbell of
the Ximenestre apartment. Mme. Ximenestre opened the
door, Rover burst in and M. Ximenestre, sobbing with
fatigue, fell into his wife's arms.

"Whatever's this?"

Mme. Ximenestre's cry was wrung from her breast.

"It's Rover," gasped M. Ximenestre, and with a desperate
effort, he added: "Merry Christmas, my dear!"

"Merry Christmas? Merry Christmas?" spluttered Mme.
Ximenestre. "What on earth are you talking about?"

"It's Christmas Eve, isn't it?" cried M. Ximenestre,

himself again now that he was back in the warmth and safety of his own home. "Well, then, here's my Christmas present to you, to you all," he added, as his children emerged wide-eyed, from the kitchen. "I'm giving you Rover. There!"

And he strode resolutely into the bedroom. Once there, however, he collapsed onto the bed and picked up his pipe, a pipe which dated from World War I and of which he was fond of saying, "It's seen a few things, I can tell you." With trembling hands he filled it and lit it, pulled the bedspread over his legs and awaited the onslaught.

Mme. Ximenestre, livid—horrifyingly livid, M. Ximenestre thought privately—entered the room almost immediately. M. Ximenestre's first reaction was that of a soldier in the trenches: he tried to bury himself completely beneath the bedspread. . . . All that could be seen of him was one of his few remaining tufts of hair and the smoke from his pipe. But this sufficed for Mme. Ximenestre's wrath:

"Would you mind telling me what this dog is supposed to be?"

"It's a kind of sheepdog, I think," M. Ximenestre's voice replied weakly.

"A kind of sheepdog?" (Mme. Ximenestre was beside herself with fury.) "And what do you think your son expected for Christmas? And your daughter? As for me,

I know I don't count. . . . But what about them? And
you bring back this frightful animal!"

Rover entered on cue. He jumped up onto M.
Ximenestre's bed, curled up beside him and laid his head
on his. Tears of tenderness, luckily hidden by the bedspread, welled up in his friend's eyes.

"It's too much," said Mme. Ximenestre. "How do you
know that the creature isn't rabid?"

"That would make two of you," M. Ximenestre said
coldly.

This shocking retort had the effect of getting rid of Mme.
Ximenestre. Rover licked his master and went to sleep.
At midnight, his wife and children went to Mass without
telling him. Feeling slightly queasy, at a quarter to one
he decided to take Rover for a short walk. He put on his
big muffler and ambled off in the direction of the church,
Rover sniffing in all the doorways.

The church was packed, and M. Ximenestre tried in vain
to push his way through the door. He had to wait outside
in the snow, his muffler up to his eyes, while the carols
of good Christians echoed in his ears. Rover pulled so
hard on his rope that in the end M. Ximenestre sat down
and attached it to his foot. Little by little, cold and
emotion numbed his already distraught mind, until he no
longer quite knew what he was doing there. So that when
the flood of faithful suddenly poured out of the church

he was taken by surprise. Before he had time to get to his feet and untie the rope, a young woman's voice cried:

"Oh, look at the lovely dog! Oh! the poor man! . . . Jean-Claude, wait."

And to M. Ximenestre's bewilderment, a five-franc piece dropped into his lap. He stood up, stammering, and the man called Jean-Claude, moved to pity, gave him a second coin and wished him a Merry Christmas.

"But," stammered M. Ximenestre, "but . . . look here . . ."

We all know how contagious charity can be. Nearly every member of the congregation who left by the north aisle of the church gave alms to M. Ximenestre and Rover. Dazed, covered in snow, M. Ximenestre tried in vain to dissuade them.

Having left by the south aisle, Mme. Ximenestre and her children returned home. M. Ximenestre arrived back shortly afterwards, apologized for his little joke earlier in the day and gave each of them a sum of money equivalent to the cost of their presents. The Christmas feast that night went off very well. Afterward, M. Ximenestre and Rover went to bed gorged with turkey, and side by side they slept the sleep of the just.

Separation Roman-style

THIS WAS THE LAST TIME HE WOULD TAKE HER TO A
cocktail party. She herself was unaware of it, but he was
about to throw her to the lions: his friends.

Tonight he was going to rid himself of this blonde,
boring, demanding, rather snobbish, insipid and not
particularly sensual woman. Tonight, at long last, after
more than two years, this decision (to which he couldn't
be said to have given mature consideration, having made
it in a moment of anger on a beach near Rome) was
about to be put into effect. Luigi, darling of hostesses,
lover of fast cars, fast women and frivolities, but cowardly
in the extreme where some other things in life were
concerned, was about to make a formal break with his

mistress. The strange thing was that he could manage it only with the help of that bevy of people, heartless and amusing and cynical (but, to him, charming, affectionate and warm), whom he called "my friends." Gradually, over the past three months, they had watched him become restive, irritated, withdrawn—more and more alienated, in fact, from poor boring Inge.

Poor boring Inge had long been one of the most beautiful women in Rome, invited "everywhere," and, indeed, as those same friends said with pride, one of the most beautiful of Luigi's mistresses.

But two years had passed, and with them fashions and God knows what else, and now Luigi was in a state of exasperation as he drove the still-beautiful—though discredited—Inge to the party in question, the farewell party. It was strange, even for him, to realize that it was no longer the woman herself he was rejecting, but the image of her. He wasn't rejecting a profile, a mouth, shoulders, hips, feet, all of which he had, in his time, adored, venerated almost (for he was a sensual man); he was rejecting a stereotype, a kind of figurine created by the remark, endlessly repeated, "Inge, you know? Luigi's girl." And try as he might, as he drove through the streets of Rome, try as he might to tell himself that she was made of flesh and blood like himself, he had the impression of traveling alongside a life-size cutout doll,

smartly dressed and propped up beside him, pointlessly, for
an indefinite journey; and yet one that had only lasted
two years and would end tonight.

He was as remote from this Swedish woman as he was
close to his Italian friends: his world, his little world of
friends, his fellow Catholics, his henchmen, his peers.
To tell the truth, he had no very clear idea why he wanted
to break with Inge on this particular evening, or why it
was necessary that everyone know about it. It was part
of that weird fatalism, that twisted morality, that was still
rife in Rome twenty centuries after Nero. Indeed, sitting
at the steering wheel of his smart convertible, loftily
disdaining to wear his seat belt, Luigi fully intended to
toss his Christian to the wild beasts of the arena. That is
to say, he was going to throw her over in such a resound-
ingly public way that the break would be irrevocable.
It wasn't that he was a contemptible man, but he had
become so dependent on the company of friends that he
developed a sort of horror of being alone, a habit of
always being with someone, and a deep-felt, almost
visceral need for the good opinion of others. "Others"
being the imbecile or the intelligent, the hardhearted or
the tenderhearted, the hunters or the hunted, but, at all
events, "other people," indefatigably patrolling the pave-
ments of their city, Rome. People morbidly self-absorbed,
self-poisoned, walking the tightrope between their vices,

their pleasures, their health and—occasionally—their affections. Inge had arrived in their midst like an object— a beautiful, blue-eyed, tall, fair, eminently elegant object— and was immediately sought after, like some desirable trophy. And it was Luigi de Santo, architect, Roman, thirty years old, with a successful past and a promising future, who had carried off the trophy, had taken it home, placed it in his bed and extracted words—even cries— of love from it; it was he who had demanded of this northern woman that she conform to the demands of southern men. Not to any special vice—Luigi was suf- ficiently unneurotic or sufficiently masculine not to have any. But time, fugitive, destructive time, had passed; Inge grew moody. The names of Stockholm and Gothenburg cropped up more and more frequently in her conversation, to which, needless to say, he hardly ever listened. He had a great deal of work. Hence, that evening, glancing at her with the eyes of a traitor, the eyes of an Iago, he was astonished and almost alarmed by his own curiosity. After all, in an hour or two he would be quitting this woman, this profile, this body, this human destiny no less, without ever having truly known them. It didn't occur to him to worry about what she would do with herself— living with a carefree, generous, rather remote man for a couple of years doesn't drive a woman, provided that she, too, is carefree, generous and remote, to suicide. No

doubt she would go off to some other Italian town—or
to Paris—and it was extremely unlikely that she would
miss him, or he her. More than anything else, they had
"cohabited," "coexisted" like two fashion plates, two
silhouettes, sketched not by themselves but by the society
they lived in; they had, to all intents and purposes, played
a theatrical role without theater, a caricatural role without
caricature, and a sentimental role without sentiment.
It was fitting that Luigi de Santo should have chosen an
ephemeral creature like Inge Ingeborg as his mistress.
It was equally fitting that they should have desired each
other, tolerated each other and then dropped each other
after two years. . . .
   She gave a little yawn, turned her head toward him and
asked in her quiet voice, with that slight accent that had
begun to get on his nerves these past two days, "who"
would be "there" tonight. And when he replied, smiling,
"the usual crowd," she suddenly looked rather downcast.
Perhaps she, too, realized that it was all over, perhaps
she, too, was beginning to break loose, to break loose from
him? The thought reawakened Luigi's atavistic male
instincts: he told himself that, if he wished, he could do
anything he liked with her: keep her, placate her, give her
ten children, lock her up and also—why not?—love her.
The idea made him chuckle, and she turned to him and
said, "You're in a good mood tonight, aren't you?" but in

a tone of voice so much more questioning than playful that he was quite taken aback. "But after all," he told himself as he drove through the Piazza di Spagna, "she must have an inkling that something's up. Carla was on the telephone to me for half an hour, and then Giana and Umberto; and even though she never listens in—not that she'd understand a word if she did, poor girl, even if she does speak Italian fluently—she must be aware that something's going on. Women's intuition, and all that." And having relegated her to the female clan, to that horde of obsessive and obsessed women of 1975, he felt slightly reassured. She was a woman whom he had looked after reasonably well, whom he had made love to adequately, whom he had taken around with him, to beaches, chalets and parties, always ready to defend her physically and—also physically, although in a different way—always ready to attack her. The fact that she never gave him a straight answer, that they seldom said to each other, "I love you," and that whenever they did, in their respective idioms, it was prompted by lust rather than sentiment and meant nothing. In any case, as Guido and Carla had said over the telephone, it was high time he got rid of her—he was getting into a rut. Two years was quite long enough for a man of his type, with his charm and originality, to be seen around with a Swedish model. And theirs was a judgment he could trust; they knew

him, knew him better than he knew himself. That had
been generally accepted from the beginning, or rather,
since he was fifteen years old.

The villa was brilliantly lit. Luigi thought wryly that
Inge's last memory of Rome would be a glamorous one.
Red and black sports cars gleamed in the rain; there was
the charming and devoted manservant running to greet
them with his multicolored umbrella; there was the worn
pale stone of the historic steps; and inside, there were all
those smartly dressed women and all those men so
obviously eager to undress them. Nevertheless, as he took
Inge's arm to escort her up the steps he had a disagreeable
feeling, as though he were leading someone to a bull-
fight, only by way of the toril, or introducing an un-
suspecting innocent to a gambling den or an orgy.

Immediately Carla was upon them (rather than merely
before them); she pounced on them. She laughed gaily;
she looked first at Inge, then at him, and laughed in
anticipation.

"My darlings," she said, "my darlings, I thought you
were never coming."

Naturally he kissed her, they both did, and then made
their way across the room. He knew Rome and Roman
society inside out, and the manner in which the crowd
parted before them to form a sort of corridor confirmed
his suspicions, his expectations: all these people were in

the know, all these people had been waiting for their arrival, all these people were aware that tonight, he, Luigi, in his usual dazzling style, planned to chuck his mistress, Inge Ingeborg from Sweden, who was admittedly very beautiful but who had been around too long.

She appeared to notice nothing. She leaned on his arm, she greeted all these dear friends, she went over to the buffet, ready (as she always was, to give her her due), to drink, eat, dance and, later on, make love. No more, no less. But it suddenly occurred to him that, while she had never offered less, perhaps it was up to him to have asked for more.

She calmly finished a vodka and tonic, and Carla eagerly advised her to have another. Imperceptibly, as though part of a badly rehearsed but rather malign chorus, the friends gathered around them in a semicircle. They were waiting . . . but for what? For him to announce to all and sundry that this woman bored him, for him to slap her face, make love to her on the spot? For what? In fact, he didn't know why, on this heavy, thundery autumn evening in Rome, he should have to explain to all these blank faces (at once so familiar and so anonymous) that it had become so necessary and so urgent for him to drop her.

He recalled that he had once said: "She's not our sort," but looking at the "sort" that surrounded them, that assortment of jackals, vultures and sheep, he wondered if he hadn't spoken more truly than he knew. Strangely, and certainly for the first time since he had known this beautiful blonde young woman from the north, who didn't belong to him yet shared his bed, he felt a sense of solidarity with her.

Giuseppe arrived, handsome and high-spirited as ever. He kissed Inge's hand with an almost theatrical flourish, and Luigi caught himself thinking that he was playacting. Then Carla returned to the fray. She asked Inge with great solemnity whether she had seen Visconti's latest film. Then Aldo blundered onto the scene and hinted to Inge that her decorative presence would always be welcome at his country place near Aosta. (Aldo was inclined to jump the gun.) Then Marina, the presiding divinity at these events, came up to them, putting one hand on Luigi's sleeve and the other on Inge's arm.

"My God," she said, "what a handsome couple! You really were made for each other. . . ."

The crowd held its breath; the corrida had begun. But the bull, the boring, placid Inge, merely smiled. Clearly this was the cue for Luigi to make some pointed remark, to do something amusing. His friends were waiting, but he couldn't think of anything. He made one of those typically Italian gestures which meant "*niente*," or "no thanks." Somewhat disappointed, Carla, who had more or less been promised a tragicomedy tonight without being told exactly where, returned to the attack.

"It's terribly hot," she said. "I imagine, Inge, my dear, that the summer is cooler where you come from. After all, if my memory serves me right, Sweden is north of here, isn't it?"

Giuseppe, Marina, Guido and the others burst out laughing. But Luigi wondered what was so funny, after all, about pointing out that Sweden was further north than Italy. Momentarily the thought crossed his mind that Carla wasn't as witty as *Vogue* made her out to be. He tried to dismiss it as unworthy, as when he was a little boy at the Jesuit school in Turin and they spoke to him about self-abuse.

"I believe Sweden is indeed further north than Italy," Inge replied in that unemphatic tone that had the effect of neutralizing everything she said, and even perhaps everything she did; but it evidently sounded irresistibly funny to someone, since there was a guffaw from among the group crowded around the buffet.

It must be nervous tension, thought Luigi. They're all waiting for me to send her packing and the cruder the language the better, and what's more, I don't see how I'm going to get out of it.

Then Inge raised her violet eyes to his—her violet eyes

had been one of the chief reasons for her instant success
in Rome—and made a remark that was astounding in
the circumstances, surrounded as she was:

"Luigi, I find this party boring. Would you mind if we
went somewhere else?"

Lightning struck, the chandeliers tinkled, the waiters
swooned, the chihuahuas went wild and the scales fell from
Luigi's eyes. Suddenly, as they looked at each other
there was a flash of understanding between these two
people, and in the truly violet, truly candid eyes of the
woman there was no longer a naïve question but an
affirmation, meaning "I love you, you idiot." And similarly,
in the brown eyes of the world-weary Roman, a naïve,
masculine, childish question: "Can it be true?" Everything
was reversed. The situation, the ideas, the characters, the
scenario and even the denouement. The "friends"
suddenly found themselves hanging from the ceiling by
their heels, doubled up like bats in winter. The crowd now
formed a triumphal way leading to an open sports car,
and Rome was as beautiful as ever. Rome was Rome, and
love was where Rome was.

The Corner Café

"IT'S PECULIAR," HE SAID TO HIMSELF AS HE WENT down the stairs from that forthright doctor's surgery, "it's peculiar to think what my feet are doing. They're taking me straight down this seedy, ordinary staircase, straight to a certain and unthinkable death."

He had watched these feet of his, these familiar feet, sometimes nimbly performing a dance step between a woman's feet, sometimes in naked repose on a beach. And now, with a sort of disgust, horror and surprise, he watched these same feet descending, step by step, that all-too-outspoken doctor's staircase. What an absurd, insensate thing death was! He, Marc, couldn't be going to die. Between the glance the doctor had given his photograph (or rather the photograph of his body, of some portion or another of it—he didn't want to know which—an obscene photograph in his opinion, an X ray) and him, himself, there had been something indefinable, unreal: an enormous hiatus, livid, pallid, stupid. It was inconceivable that between the Marc who had run up this staircase, late, out of breath and even worried about his heart, and the Marc who was coming down those same stairs quietly, mortally, at once conscious and unconscious of his fate—it was inconceivable that between the two of them no more than half an hour had passed. Half an hour with a cold, saddened, polite man, sympathetic in his very coldness. "Three months," he had said, "the lungs, you know . . ." And Marc, whose imminent death no one would ever have suspected, or even desired, Marc felt his skin crawl at the idea of such exactitude: *I, me, myself, I am going to die.*

And yet he had done all he could to force the doctor into this unaccustomed honesty, still unfashionable in Europe. He had certainly told him that he and his wife were separated, that his parents were senile, and that none of the children he might have fathered had any legal claim on him. It was no doubt because of these over-simplifications that he had received so formal a death sentence. Perhaps, after all, doctors did have a certain distaste for their more disreputable patients. And he was cerainly disreputable. Thank God, his cancer was in the right place! Some cancers were ignominious: cancer of the colon, of the skin and other bits of one's insides. His was reserved for the élite: his would be a classic death, within three months, from lung cancer. He began to laugh to himself, feeling young and jaunty and in the swim. He cackled, almost triumphantly, at the thought that he might, after all, have had cancer of the intestine. That would have been much harder, much trickier to talk about—always assuming he had been prepared to admit it in the first place. What euphemism would he have found with which to disguise that faintly ridiculous organ, universally associated with infantile diarrhea and exotic diseases? He was lucky in his misfortune. For once there would be no need to make excuses, to dot the *i*'s and cross the *t*'s: he would be able to say, "It's killing me," without exaggeration. No longer would he have to say, "If I'm leaving you, it's because of this" or, "If I'm going, it's because of that," the *this* and *that* being both untrue. For once he wouldn't have to retreat behind the weak line of his sensitivity or the strong line of his vanity; he wouldn't even have to apologize for his death.

He reached the final bend in the staircase and suddenly Life, with a capital *L*, appeared before him on the threshold, and he paused for a moment. Outside there was such bright sunlight, but already he visualized himself shivering in the darkness of the sickroom, surrounded by reassuring friends and deliberating doctors. Already the sun was a sunflower, one vast regret, and it must have been the sight of it that gave Marc an access of true courage, possibly for the first time in his life. He rushed out to the street like a man possessed; confronted the boulevard, the bustle, the city; and stood there for a moment on the curb, like a deaf-mute, before walking calmly toward the café on the corner. A café he had never noticed before, but which he knew would be engraved on his memory forever; and then he realized that "forever" meant three months, and that the whole thing was absurd, repulsive, grotesque and melodramatic.

It surprised him that his thoughts had not turned to anyone in particular. After all, at times like these a girl will turn to her mother, a man to his wife and a mythomaniac to his destiny. But he had no one and nowhere to go to, except to this typical café with its formica, its workmen and its beer. He propped himself up against the bar and for a moment he experienced that old familiar, comfortable feeling he had always had when he settled in like this alone against a slab of wood or marble. There weren't many customers, and he saw this

as providential. He beckoned to the waiter, who came
scudding toward him like a ship under sail, and ordered
a Pernod. Why? he didn't know: he had always detested
the taste of aniseed. Then he realized that its smell
reminded him of beaches, women's bodies, shellfish,
seaweed, bouillabaisse, swimming, and that this smell had
become, in a way, the smell of life itself. He might equally
well have asked the waiter to bring him a Calvados, and
with it lawns and promenades, storms and windswept
avenues. He might also have asked for barley water: his
mother's breast, her hair and the smell of damp wood, in
"their" bedroom, when he was a child. He might also have
asked for a glass of Chanel No. 5 (Anne), Femme by
Rochas (Heidi), Vent Vert by . . . What was her name,
that girl? And then there was the smell of his own tears,
caused by a whiff of that Guerlain worn by that woman
he had never seen again, and who was called . . . Inès?
It was incredible, the potency of a street, a perfume, an
atmosphere, in Paris. It was amazing how all these people
in this bar were at one and the same time old friends and
total strangers. He hadn't intentionally done much that
might give him cause for regret. He had knocked around,
as they say, casually and inoffensively, from one objective
to another, one bed to another, one love affair to another.
Always bruising himself, tearing himself to pieces, never

insensitive, never blasé, sometimes cynical, even more often smitten, flapping like an aging gull behind the same tractors, but never tired of following them.

Yes, he had been a bit of a fool, ready for anything, but really, when it came down to it, he didn't have anything much to be ashamed of, and the fact that his death was tangible and predetermined didn't seem to him a disgrace. He must accelerate it, that's all, get it over with, so as not to have to suffer himself as he would inevitably become: bedraggled, bald and tottering from one injection to the next. No, he couldn't face that, and yet he wasn't so sure that he would have the guts to prevent it. And then he became his cavalier, charming, engaging self once more, lovable old Marc, and he raised his glass to the bartender in a grandiloquent, rather ridiculous gesture.

"Say, old pal," he said in a ringing voice, bringing conversation to a halt, and causing the dozen or so customers, including the mandatory pair of lovers, to stare at him in amazement. "Say, I want to pay for a round of drinks for everyone. I've just won the jackpot at Saint Cloud."

There was a moment of mild astonishment, which quickly turned to gaiety, and everyone, that is, the dozen or so people there—his last witnesses—applauded him enthusiastically. They all drank to one another's health—

including his own—then he paid the bill punctiliously
and returned to his car, which was parked at the entrance
to the doctor's.

As he was still reasonably fit, he had the strength as
well as the decency to crash into a tree, as though by
accident, just before reaching Mantes-la-Jolie, and there,
as the saying goes, he came to rest.

The Seven O'Clock Fix

"HOLD IT A MINUTE!"

Cecily B., the actress, was beautiful, stupid and stubborn as a mule.

"I'm sorry," she cried in the husky voice that had taken both London and Broadway by storm, "I'm sorry, Dick, but I just don't see the character of Petulia like that. . . ."

Sitting alone in the front row of the orchestra, Dick gave a slight shrug of the shoulders.

"And I may add," continued the rasping voice from the brightly lit stage, "that in my opinion this woman isn't even a tart."

Much to his own surprise (and choking back his laughter), Dick Leighton, one of the best playwrights of the day—or at least considered to be so—began to argue the point.

"But, my dear," he managed to say, "my dear, dear Cecily, I've never for one moment suggested . . ."

She cut him short immediately with one of those famous withering gestures of hers, which, as a rule, effectively silenced the opposition.

"You've insinuated as much," she snapped.

Dick turned and smiled at his old friend Reginald, whom he hadn't seen for a long time, not since Oxford, in fact, and who was looking even more asinine than usual.

It seemed to him that his friend's face, glowing faintly in the darkness three rows behind, reflected an image of the audience to come, and he had the impression that he, too, was exasperated by the tirades and antics of Miss Cecily B.

"What do you think?" whispered Dick.

By way of reply, Reginald gave a huge, almost ribald guffaw, which clearly meant: "That bitch! Bring her to heel! Tell her to go to hell! By Jove, you've got to do something!"

For Dick, it was an odd situation. He had never worked with anyone except professionals. Now, out of the blue, he found himself with this old friend whom he had met by chance, who didn't understand a thing, treated everything as a joke and, funnily enough, never let you get away with anything. In other words, with an untypical example of the typical theatergoer—as though there was such a thing! Certainly, even so long after Oxford, Reginald still exercised the same absurd hold over him, based solely on conventional views and a loud voice.

"Well, then," said Cecily, "what's the verdict, Dick darling?"

"The verdict is that you're a pain in the neck," replied Dick. "There was never any question of a tart in the play . . . and there won't be any bossy actresses either."

And suddenly a new silence filled his ears. He saw the director and the stage manager jump to their feet, silhouetted against the footlights; he saw a sort of panic-stricken shadow play on stage. Then behind him he heard his old classmate, the clownish Reginald, applauding for all he was worth. Amazing, the noise he made with his clapping! A heartwarming, deafening sound, the very sound he had dreamed of for the past ten years, sincere and quite inappropriate, the right sound in the wrong place.

And all at once he realized how out of place he himself was, between this fool of an actress and this fool of a director, Arnold. Straddling the pair of them, flitting from one to the other, almost tottering with fatigue in his efforts to explain the meaning of his play to one and the way to play it to the other. Reduced nightly, through sheer nervous tension, to tearing his hair, sitting up late with friends, lying awake in bed asking himself why he was alive and what the secret of his survival was, money or no money.

That explosive, exploding laugh from Reginald, asinine, brotherly Reginald, had aroused him from a somber, gilded, troubled dream, magnificent but insubstantial. He had honestly believed in that interplay of light and shade, objects and gestures, movements and images, that in the end added up to what he was trying to say. He had believed in the curtain going up and the lights going down, in criticisms as well as compliments—he had even believed that he had friends and enemies. He had believed that, where he was concerned, other people were divided into distinct camps: bastards to the right, chums to the left. He had believed that what he said mattered to the world at large. But now, suddenly, caught between the innate ferocity of the illustrious Cecily and the easygoing nature, not to say heartiness, of the ebullient Reginald, he felt that he was being put on the spot, goaded by something outside himself, something he couldn't define: an abstract entity. Whether it was style or intelligence or perfection or love, he failed to connect it with either of these two faces, close as they were to him, the one in the glare of the lights, the other in shadow.

"That's theater," he said to himself halfheartedly. For

he had reached that point of success combined with exhaustion when whatever you say to yourself is said halfheartedly.

He raised his hand in an authoritative gesture, or at least he hoped and assumed it was authoritative, accompanied by a shrill whistle, and the houselights came up. The theater once more became a theater of red and gold and black. Cecily broke off her harangue and, submissively, Dick led Reginald to the foot of the stage and up the steps. Reginald was bronzed and very handsome in a coarse kind of way, and Dick, introducing them, could see that Cecily was aware of it. Then, slightly nauseated by his play, his characters, even this theater rustling in anticipation with ideas, silks, satins, sighs and possibly tears, Dick walked unsteadily backstage, sensing the director's eyes following him. Already he could hear the man's flat, boring Freudian psychological interpretation of his play. The very opposite, in other words, of what he had intended and above all what he had hoped for from this final rehearsal. So, as a precautionary measure, since he had his kit with him, he went into the lavatory, put a tourniquet around his arm, and gave himself his regular injection of heroin.

He emerged briskly three minutes later, and it was with every appearance of delight that he rejoined his charming cast and his old Oxford friend, floating amiably about in the wings. Everything was fine, couldn't be better. After all, one shouldn't ask too much of an old war-horse like Cecily B., any more than one should of a hollow-eyed young dog like himself.

Italian
Skies

THE EVENING WAS DRAWING NEAR. THE SKY SEEMED TO be dying between Miles' eyelids. Only a white line above the hill remained, squeezed between his lashes and the dark mass of the hillside.

Miles sighed, stretched out his hand to the table and grasped the bottle of brandy. It was good French brandy, golden and warm to the throat. Other spirits made him feel cold and he avoided them. Brandy was the only one . . . But it was his fourth or fifth, and his wife protested.

"Miles! Please! You're drunk as it is. And quite incapable of holding a racket. We can't invite the Simesters to make up a four at tennis and then leave them to play on their own. Don't you think you've had enough?"

Without relinquishing the bottle, Miles closed his eyes, suddenly weary. Unutterably weary.

"My dear Margaret," he began, "if you only realized . . ."

But he stopped. She could never realize how weary he felt, after ten years of playing tennis, exchanging "hellos," slapping people on the back and reading the newspapers at his club.

"Here they are," said Margaret. "Do try and behave. People in our position . . ."

Miles raised himself on one elbow and looked at the Simesters. He was tall, thin and red-faced, with a supercilious, intolerant air. She was muscular, hideously muscular, in Miles' opinion. Margaret, too, was getting that way: outdoor life, ear-to-ear grin, mannish laugh and hearty camaraderie. Nauseated, he sank back into his wicker chair. In this corner of Scotland there was nothing human except the gentle line of the hills, the warmth of the brandy and himself. Everything else was—he tried to think of a pejorative term—everything else was "organized." Pleased with his choice of epithet, he glanced at his wife. Then, in spite of himself, he began to speak:

"When I was serving in the Italian and French campaigns . . ."

His voice sounded odd. He felt Simester's eyes on him

and guessed what he was thinking: Poor old Miles, he's cracking up, he ought to take up polo again and stop drinking that poisonous stuff. It angered him, and he continued in a louder voice:

"In Italy and the south of France, women don't play tennis. In certain districts of Marseille, they stand in doorways and watch you walk down the street. If you stop and speak to one of them, and you've made a mistake, she'll say, '*Va-t-en.*' "

He pronounced "*Va-t-en*" in a comical way.

"But if you haven't made a mistake, she'll say, '*Viens.*' "

And the way he pronounced "*Viens,*" almost intimately, wasn't comical at all. Simester opened his mouth to intervene, then closed it again. The two women had become rather flushed.

"They don't go in for sport," Miles went on, as if talking to himself, "and so they're soft and tender, like apricots in September. They don't belong to clubs, they belong to men, or a man. They spend their time talking in the sun and their skin tastes of the sun and their voices are husky. And they absolutely never say 'hello.'

"Of course, we say it all the time," he added gloomily. "But whatever it is about those southern women I knew, I like them better than the sour, flat-chested creatures around here with their golf clubs and their emancipation."

And he poured himself a large glass of brandy. There

was a stunned silence. Simester tried in vain to think of
something amusing to say. Margaret's eyes were fixed
on her husband with an expression of outrage. He looked
up:

"No need to get worked up, Margaret. I didn't know
you in 1944."

"You needn't tell us about your wartime pickups, Miles.
I trust our friends will excuse . . ."

But Miles was no longer listening. He had walked off
to the far end of the garden, his bottle in his hand. Away
from tennis courts, voices and faces. He was a little
unsteady on his feet, but it was a pleasant sensation. It
was pleasanter still when he stretched out on the grass,
with the earth spinning like a top beneath him. A gigantic
top smelling of hay. The earth everywhere had the same
sweet scent. Miles closed his eyes and inhaled. He inhaled
an aroma that was very old and very far away, the smell
of a town, and of the sea that bathed it, the smell of a
seaport.

Where was it? Naples? Marseille? Miles had served in
the two campaigns with the Americans. In a jeep driven
at a crazy speed by an American Negro. One day the
jeep had left the road with a prodigious leap, with an iron
clatter that had deafened him, and he had found himself
in a field, in among the wheat, hardly daring to breathe
for fear of frightening away his life before he could

renew acquaintance with it. He couldn't move, and there
was a smell that he recognized with a mixture of disgust
and curious pleasure: the smell of blood. The wheat
stalks waved gently above his head, silhouetted against
an Italian sky that was blue to the point of pallor. He
had moved his hand and brought it up to his eyes to
shield them from the sun. And feeling his eyelids beneath
his hand, his palm brushed by his lashes, suddenly
feeling through this double contact that he, Miles, was
there, and that he was alive, he fainted for the second time.

He wasn't in a fit state to be moved far. They took
him to a farmhouse, which, at first sight, he had thought
rather dirty. His legs hurt him badly; he was afraid that
he might never be able to walk again, let alone play
tennis or golf. He said over and over again to his com-
manding officer: "To think I was the best golfer at my
college!" Miles was twenty-two years old. They installed
him in a hayloft and left him there with his leg in a
plaster cast. A small window looked onto the fields, the
peaceful plain, the sky. Miles was afraid.

The Italian women who looked after him spoke scarcely
a word of English. It was a week before Miles noticed
that the younger of the two had dark, extremely dark,
eyes, that her skin was golden and that she was rather
plump. She looked about thirty, or maybe less, and her
husband had been taken prisoner by the Americans. He

had been forcibly conscripted, the old mother said, and
she wept, clawing her hair and tearing her handkerchief.
Miles was deeply embarrassed by such a display of
emotion: he felt it wasn't suitable. But to please the old
woman, he told her that there was nothing to worry about,
that her son wouldn't remain a prisoner of war for long,
and that no one knew what was happening anymore. The
young woman smiled without saying a word. She had
very white teeth and she didn't chatter gaily about school
like the girls he knew. She hardly spoke to him at all,
and something gradually built up between them that
disturbed and embarrassed him. That, too, wasn't proper.
Those pregnant silences, those half-smiles, those sidelong
glances. But he didn't tell *her* that he no longer knew
what was happening.

One day, the tenth after his arrival, she was sitting
beside him, knitting. From time to time she asked him
if he wanted something to drink, for it was very hot.
But he always refused. His legs were very painful, and
he wondered if he would ever be able to play tennis with
Gladys and the others again. He agreed with some
reluctance to hold her wool between his wrists while she
wound it rapidly into a ball, keeping her eyes lowered.
She had very long eyelashes. Miles noticed them briefly,
before he reverted to his own gloomy thoughts: what

on earth would he do at the tennis club if he should
become a cripple?

"Please?" she said imploringly.

He had let his wrists drop. He raised them again at once
with a word of apology, and she smiled at him. Miles
smiled back at her, then looked away. Gladys used to
say . . . But he couldn't keep his mind on Gladys. He
watched the skein of wool gradually diminish between
his wrists. He thought vaguely that when she had finished
she would no longer be like this, half leaning over him,
in her brightly-colored blouse. And involuntarily he
slowed her down by twisting his wrists. Finally he seized
the tail end of the wool in his fist and clung to it. He
thought confusedly, Just a joke, a little joke.

When she came to the end of the wool and could go no
further because of Miles, she raised her eyes. Miles sensed
his own gaze faltering, and he attempted a foolish grin.
She tugged gently at the wool, very gently, in order not
to break it, and so found herself right up against Miles,
who closed his eyes. She kissed him slowly while
detaching the wool from his fingers as if he were a child.
And Miles let it happen, filled with an unbelievable
sense of bliss and sweetness. When he opened his eyes,
the sun made him close them again immediately against
the crimson blouse. The young woman cradled his head in

her hand the way the Italians cradle the wicker covering of their Chianti flasks when drinking.

Miles stayed on his own in the hayloft. For the first time he was conscious of being happy and at home in this sun-scorched land. Lying on his side, he could see the wheatfields and olive groves, he could feel the moist touch of the young woman's mouth on his lips, and it seemed to him that he had lived in this place for centuries.

Now this young woman stayed with him the whole day. The old woman no longer came up there. Miles' legs improved, he ate little aromatic goat cheeses and Luigia had fixed a flask of Chianti above his bed so that he only had to tip it up to receive a jet of rough dark-red wine down his throat. The sun flooded the loft. He would kiss Luigia for whole afternoons on end, resting his head on her crimson-covered breast, thinking of nothing, not even of Gladys and his friends at the club.

One day the major returned in a jeep, and with him discipline. He examined Miles' legs, removed the plaster cast and made him walk a few steps. He told Miles he could leave the next day, that someone would come to fetch him and that he mustn't forget to thank the Italian family.

For a moment Miles was alone in the loft. He felt he should be much more pleased than he was to be cured, since he could now play tennis, golf, shoot with his

father's friends and fox-trot with Gladys or some other
girl. He could stride around London and Edinburgh to
his heart's content. And yet the sun-soaked fields, the
empty flask of Chianti over his bed, filled him with
absurd regrets. It really was time he left! In any case,
Luigia's husband would soon be back. He had done
nothing wrong with her, only kissed her a few times. He
suddenly thought that tonight, now that he was better
and no longer imprisoned in plaster, he might know
more of Luigia than her mouth and her gentleness.

She returned to the loft. She laughed to see him standing
up, a bit shaky on his legs. Then her laughter died away
and she looked at him anxiously, like a child. Miles
hesitated, then nodded:

"I'm leaving tomorrow, Luigia," he said.

He repeated the sentence slowly two or three times to
make sure that she understood. He saw her look away and
he felt appallingly helpless and boorish. Luigia looked at
him again and then, without a word, removed her
crimson blouse. Her shoulders gleamed in the sunlight,
then in the grateful shadows of Miles' bed.

The next day, when it was time for him to leave, she
wept. Sitting in the jeep, Miles saw the young woman
weeping and, behind her, the fields and trees he had looked
at for so long from his bed. Miles said "Good-bye, good-
bye" and tried to remember the musty smell of the

loft and the abandoned Chianti flask hanging at the end of its string over the bed. He gazed in despair at the dark-haired young woman. He shouted that he would never forget her, but she didn't understand.

And then there had been Naples and the Neapolitan women, some of whom were called Luigia. And later the return journey through the south of France. While all his fellow officers, impatient to be home, returned to England by the first available boat, Miles had lingered on for a month in the sun between the Italian and Spanish borders. He didn't dare return to see Luigia. If her husband was there he would guess, and if he wasn't, would he, Miles, be able to resist the sun-drenched fields, the old farmhouse, Luigia's kisses? Could he, with his background, end up as a peasant on an Italian plain? Miles walked endlessly along the shores of the Mediterranean, lay on the sand, drank brandy.

All that was forgotten once he was back home. Gladys meanwhile married John. Miles played tennis, but less well than before, and he had his hands full taking over from his father. Margaret was charming, loyal and cultivated. A perfect lady, in fact....

Miles opened his eyes again, seized the brandy bottle and took a long swig from it. He was becoming gradually redder in the face and more and more dehydrated from

the effects of alcohol. That morning, he had watched a
blood vessel burst in his left eye. Luigia would be very fat
by now, and blowsy. And the loft would be deserted.
And Chianti would never taste the same again. There
was no alternative but to carry on as usual. Office, lunch,
political news in the paper, *what do you think, Sidney,
old boy?* Office, the car, *hello, Margaret,* and Sunday in
the country with the Simesters or the Joneses, eighteen
holes of golf, *soda or water?* And, more often than not,
that interminable rain. And, thank God, brandy.

The bottle was empty. Miles threw it away and got
laboriously to his feet. He felt embarrassed at returning
to face the others. Why that outburst? It simply wasn't
proper! It was undignified. He suddenly remembered
how the Italians would hurl insults at one another from
across the road, threatening with the most appalling
curses to kill one another, without even having the energy
to get to their feet. He laughed out loud, then suddenly
stopped. What on earth was he doing, laughing to
himself on his own lawn?

He would go back to his wicker chair; he would say
"Sorry" in an offhand way and Simester would say "Think
nothing of it, old boy" with polite reserve. And no more
would be said. He could never talk to anyone about the
skies of Italy, Luigia's kisses, and the sweetness of being
helpless and bedridden in a strange house. The war had

been over for ten years. And to be honest, he was no longer either handsome or young.

He walked slowly back to the others. Tactfully, they pretended not to have noticed his absence and brought him into the conversation by degrees. Miles talked cars with Simester, declaring that Jaguars were unbeatable for speed and the ideal sports car. And then they agreed that the Australians were bound to win the Davis Cup. But secretly he was thinking of the bottle of brandy, golden and warm, that slumbered in his cupboard. And he smiled at the thought that soon he would be alone with his memories, his sunlit, tender memories, when the Simesters had left with Margaret in time to see the last film at the local cinema. When he had pretended that he had work to do and they had disappeared down the drive, and he had opened the door of his cupboard and rediscovered Italy there.

The Sun
Also Sets

THE CROWD ROARED, THEN FELL SILENT, AND IN THE
religious hush Juan Alvarez executed his eighth veronica.
The bull staggered momentarily, dazed either by the sun,
the shouting or the silence. And Lady Brighton, sitting
in the front row of the President's box, fixed her blue
eyes on him for an instant. He's brave, she thought, brave
but exhausted. Juan will make short work of him. Then
she turned back to her neighbor, the American consul
in Barcelona, and resumed her conversation about Andy
Warhol.

The time had come for the kill, and Juan skipped
forward in the sunlight, eager and assured, poised on the
tips of his toes, hurrying to meet this bull, she thought

mockingly, exactly as he hurried toward her bed in order
to spear her, agile, virile, male. "El Macho." Suddenly
she saw in her mind's eye the big four-poster bed in the
Madrid hotel where she stopped from time to time like
some Hemingway heroine, and remembered Juan skipping
forward in his suit of lights toward the wide expanse of
sheets where she lay on her back, offering herself, almost
as inoffensive as the black bull down there. She felt an
urge to laugh. Men's ideas about virility were really
rather comical. It took Juan no longer to impale her in
the act of love than to impale this bull in the act of
death; and while it was all very well for the crowd to
applaud him, for her to applaud him also was another
matter—hardly a matter for discussion, though, even with
her neighbor, the consul, knowledgeable though he
seemed on the subject of sexual relations. "Bravo!" cried
the consul noncommittally, while the "*Olés*" rose into
the raw blue sky, hats rippled like a sea of straw and
the bull fell like a ton of lead at Juan's feet. The matador
executed a graceful pirouette, turned toward her and
swept off his *montera*; whereupon the crowd rose to its
feet in tribute to this young man who was risking his
life, or rather, had apparently risked it for the sake of a
beautiful young woman. She, too, rose lightly from her
seat, smiling both at the delirious crowd and at her
lover standing triumphant over the dead beast; and she

bowed as she smiled, just as she had been taught to do
when she was a child in Virginia.

Once the arena had been cleared, the trumpets sounded
again and to the great delight of the crowd, another
black cannonball drummed against the door of the *toril*.
The door was raised and the bull catapulted into the arena
to a unanimous roar of approval, pleasure and fear. It
was a dangerous-looking brute and the young man who
advanced to meet it seemed to be thinking the same thing.
He edged toward it, the cape held firmly on his arm.
After a moment, a subdued murmur rose from the crowd
as though in disapproval of the timid bravado or the
pretended audacity of this fair-haired youth, a *torero* new
to Barcelona called Rodriguez Serra.

"His name is Rodriguez Serra," the consul informed
Lady Brighton, who nodded in acknowledgment, as to
an item of minor significance. And yet her eyes were
following every movement of the blond head, the
shoulders hunched in fear, the rigid hips, of this youth
who was facing for the first time both the tender mercies
of the crowd and the fury and apathy of a bull in front
of that same crowd. Rodriguez Serra stamped his foot
from a respectful distance; the bull took no notice;
laughter rippled here and there amongst the crowd. He
took three, four, five paces toward the bull and repeated
the performance; but either through bad luck or bad

acoustics, or for lack of wind or blood, the bull refused to
budge and continued to turn its back on him. Now the
entire crowd was convulsed with laughter. Two peons
sprang forward. But this bull seemed suddenly to have
turned to stone, standing with its eyes fixed on the door
through which it had come, as though some powerful
instinct of survival could catapult it back there. "*Toro!*"
cried the voice of the fair-haired youth. The bull turned
its head and stared at him, then walked slowly and
peaceably toward the wooden door from which it had just
emerged.

Nothing could have been plainer: the bull was quietly
dreaming of hills, heifers, luscious grass, oaks and
chestnuts, the wide-open spaces. Quite clearly, it was
dreaming of anything but this fair-haired youth, who was
supposed to bring about its death or his own sometime
within the next ten minutes. The young man, seemingly
abashed and at a loss, took a few steps toward the bull,
and the crowd, astonished at this dillydallying, suddenly
became riled and began to whistle. As though this youth
should have had a quiverful of arrows with which to
bombard the placid beast facing him, or as though he
should have leaped astride the huge black bull, or as
though, perhaps, the crowd itself felt cheated of the
savagery, the blood and the vicarious danger for which it
had paid so much. Lady Brighton's hand had reached

instinctively for her neighbor's binoculars. She was now
studying the profile of the blond and (in the consul's
opinion) obviously useless torero with remarkable interest.
The bull turned around for the third time, stared at its
adversary and (as though out of politeness) headed
toward him at a friendly, almost frolicsome canter, so that
the fair-haired youth had only to sidestep, like a fencer,
in order to avoid the near-ton-weight bearing down on
him. He shook his muleta from a distance of thirty feet:
the bull didn't budge. Then fifteen feet: still the bull
didn't budge. And suddenly the crowd fell silent, as if
mesmerized. Not by the boy's daring, which wasn't
daring at all, but by the bull's nonchalance—though it
wasn't the first time such a thing had been seen in this
arena—and the understanding that prevailed between
man and beast, their nonchalance, their indifference and
their apparent unwillingness to kill each other. Now
the *picadores*, the *banderilleros* and the entire *cuadrilla*
intervened. But no one succeeded in breaking the mute
but flagrant pact between the blond youth and the black
beast. There were a few halfhearted passes, which were
greeted with fierce whistles. There were a few pauses—
met with even fiercer whistles—and then there was the
moment when, beneath a hail of missiles, seat cushions,
tomatoes, flowers and bottles, the young man asked that
the beast's life be spared; and in so doing, renounced his

life as a torero forever, standing bareheaded, holding his *montera* before him and gazing straight into Lady Brighton's blue eyes.

"I've never seen that happen before," the President of the corrida said to the consul. "I've never seen anything like it in my life! He's not a man, that fellow. . . ."

And he stood up, signaling a reprieve on the one hand and a reproof on the other, secretly delighted to be able to punish a fellow-Spaniard's lack of manliness in front of foreigners. It was then that Lady Brighton leaned toward him and said smilingly over the consul's shoulder, not a hair out of place:

"I've never seen a man like this Rodriguez before, either—in bed, I mean. You know, I made him promise not to fool around with these creatures anymore. . . ."

And she nodded toward the black beast setting off happily on its way to its pastures, and the fair-haired young man setting off happily on his way to her bed.

The Lake of Loneliness

PRUDENCE—FOR SUCH WAS HER NAME, ALAS, AND
an inappropriate one at that—Prudence Delvaux had
parked her car in a forest path, near Trappes, and was
strolling aimlessly in the damp, chill November wind.
It was five o'clock and growing dark: a melancholy hour,
in a melancholy month, in a melancholy landscape, but
nonetheless she whistled as she walked, stooping now and
then to pick up a chestnut or a russet leaf whose color
appealed to her. She wondered dryly what she was doing
there—why, on her way home from a charming
weekend, with charming friends, with her charming lover,
she had felt a sudden and almost irresistible urge to stop
her Fiat and set off on foot on this heartrending autumn

evening, why she had suddenly succumbed to the desire
to be alone and walk.

She was wearing a silk scarf and an extremely well cut
coat in loden cloth the color of the leaves, she was
thirty years old and her handsewn walking shoes made
every stride a pleasure. A rook flew cawing overhead
and was immediately joined by a bevy of its fellows until
they filled the sky to the horizon. And oddly enough, this
raucous cry, familiar though it was, made her heart beat
faster, as though in response to some nameless terror.
Not that Prudence was afraid of prowlers, or the cold, or
the wind, or even of life itself. On the contrary, her
friends would burst out laughing whenever they uttered
her name. Considering her attitude toward life, they said,
it was the purest paradox. However, she hated anything
she couldn't understand, and that was really the only
thing she was frightened of: not understanding what was
happening to her. And now, suddenly, she had to stop
and catch her breath.

The landscape reminded her of a Brueghel, and she
liked Brueghel; she liked the warm car that awaited her
and the music she would switch on once she was back
inside it; she liked the thought of meeting, around eight
o'clock, a man who loved her and whom she loved in
return, a man called Jean-François. She also liked the
thought of getting up, yawning, after their night of love,

and gulping down the cup of coffee that he, or she, would have made for "the other"; and also the thought of her office tomorrow morning, of discussing advertising ideas with Marc, the good friend with whom she had worked for the past five years. They would agree, laughing, that, in the end, the best way of promoting a new washing powder was to show that it washed grayer, and that people needed grayness more than whiteness, dullness more than sparkle, obsolescence more than durability.

She liked all that; in fact, she liked her life: plenty of friends, plenty of lovers, an amusing job, a child even, together with a taste for music, books, flowers and log fires. But now this rook had flown over, chased by that frantic rabble, and something was tearing at her heart, something that she couldn't quite grasp, couldn't explain, not even (and this was the worst part) to herself.

The path branched to the right. There was a signboard proclaiming "*Etangs de Hollande.*" The idea of those lakes in the setting sun, with reeds, furze, perhaps some duck, immediately attracted her and she quickened her step. She came upon the first of the promised lakes almost at once. It was a mixture of blues and grays, and although not covered with wildfowl (there wasn't even a single duck) it was nevertheless strewn with dead leaves, which were slowly sinking, one after another, in a dying spiral; and each one seemed to be in need of aid and protection.

Each of these dead leaves was an Ophelia. Spotting a dead tree trunk, no doubt abandoned by a careless forester, she sat down on it. Increasingly she asked herself what she was doing there. She would end up by being late, Jean-François would be worried; he would be furious and he would be quite right. When one is happy, when one is doing what one likes to do—and also when other people like one—one has no right to sit about on tree trunks, alone, in the cold, beside a lake no one has ever heard of. It wasn't as though she was at all "neurotic," as "other people" say when talking of unhappy people (or at any rate, people who couldn't cope with life).

As though to reassure herself, she took a packet of cigarettes from her coat pocket, was relieved to discover a lighter in the other pocket, and lit up. The smoke was warm and acrid, and the cigarette tasted unfamiliar. And yet it was the same brand that she had been smoking for ten years.

"Perhaps," she said to herself, "all I really needed was to be alone for a bit. Perhaps it's been too long since I was alone. Perhaps this lake has an evil spirit. Perhaps it wasn't chance, but fate, that led me here. Perhaps there's a long history of charms and spells surrounding these lakes...."

She put her hand on the tree trunk at the point where her hip rested against it, and felt the contact of the rough

wood, worn and mellowed by rain and by solitude (for
what could be more solitary or more melancholy than
a dead tree, cut down, abandoned, no good for anything;
not as firewood, nor as timber, nor as a lovers' seat?). The
contact with the wood aroused a sort of tenderness and
affection in her, and to her astonishment she felt the tears
well up in her eyes. She contemplated the wood, the
veins of the wood, difficult though they were to make out:
gray, almost white, in wood that had itself turned gray
and white (like old people's veins, she thought: one
can't see the blood flowing, one knows it's there but one
can't see it any more than one can hear it). And it was
much the same with this tree: the sap had dried up; the
sap, the incentive, the fever, the desire to *do*, to *act*, to
act the fool, make love, create, make things happen. . . .
   All these ideas went through her head in a flash; resigned, passive, she hardly knew who she was any longer.
She, who never saw herself, who never even wanted to
see herself, whose life was full, now suddenly saw herself
as a woman in a smart coat, smoking a cigarette, sitting
on a dead tree trunk beside a stagnant lake. There was
someone inside her who wanted desperately to get away
from this place, to go back to the car, to the music in the
car, to the road and the thousand and one ways of
avoiding death, the thousand and one tricks a clever
motorist must know to avoid accidents, someone who

longed to be back in Jean-François' arms, or in a Paris café with "the grin, the gypsies, the siphons and the electricity" so dear to the heart of Guillaume Apollinaire. But there was someone else inside her whom she didn't recognize—at least whom she had never met until now— who wanted to stay until nightfall, watching the darkness settle on the lake and feeling the wood grow cold beneath her hand. And perhaps—why not?—this someone would later want to walk into that water, aware of the cold at first, then, immersing herself in it, losing herself in it, go down to the deepest depths to rejoin, on the blue and golden sands, the dead leaves that had been sucked down there throughout the day. And there, stretched out on a bed of leaves, surrounded by tender, playful fishes, this someone would be perfectly at peace at last, restored to the cradle, restored to real life, or rather to death.

I'm going crazy, she thought, and a voice whispered to her: "I assure you it's the truth, your truth," and it seemed to be the voice of childhood. And another voice, a voice acquired over thirty years of pleasure of one kind or another, said: "My dear girl, what you ought to do is to go home and take some Vitamin B or C. There's something the matter with you."

Needless to say, it was the second voice that prevailed. Prudence Delvaux stood up, abandoning the tree trunk, the lake, the leaves and life. She returned to Paris, to her divans, her bars, to what is known as existence. She returned to her love, who was known as Jean-François.

And she switched on the music in her car and she drove very carefully and she even smiled at her half hour of aberration. But it took her two months to forget the *Etangs de Hollande*. At least. And not once did she mention them to Jean-François.